D0369723

MY
LIFE
AS A
RHOMBUS

For Heather, wherever you are.

Varian Johnson

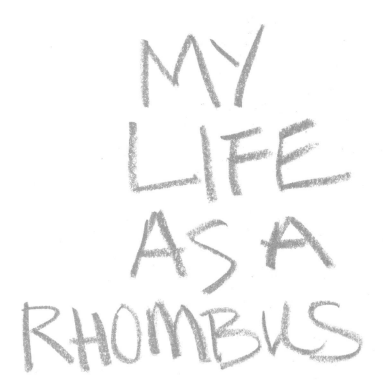

MY
LIFE
AS A
RHOMBUS

flux
™
Woodbury, Minnesota

WILLIAMSBURG REGIONAL LIBRARY
7770 CROAKER ROAD
WILLIAMSBURG, VIRGINIA 23188

FEB   2008

My Life as a Rhombus © 2007 by Varian Johnson. All rights reserved. No part of this book may be used or reproduced in any manner whatsoever, including Internet usage, without written permission from Flux except in the case of brief quotations embodied in critical articles and reviews.

First Edition
First Printing, 2007

Book design by Steffani Sawyer
Cover design by Ellen Dahl
Cover image © 2007 Image Source/PunchStock
Editing by Rhiannon Ross

Flux, an imprint of Llewellyn Publications

The Cataloging-in-Publication Data for *My Life as a Rhombus* is on file at the Library of Congress.

ISBN-13: 978-0-7387-1160-7

This is a work of fiction. Names, characters, places, and incidents are either the product of the author's imagination or are used fictitiously, and any resemblance to actual persons, living or dead, business establishments, events, or locales is entirely coincidental. Cover model(s) used for illustrative purposes only and may not endorse or represent the book's subject.

Flux
A Division of Llewellyn Worldwide, Ltd.
2143 Wooddale Drive, Dept. 978-0-7387-1160-7
Woodbury, MN 55125-2989, U.S.A.
www.fluxnow.com

Printed in the United States of America

Acknowledgements

To date, this is the hardest novel I've ever written. It would have never made it to publication without the help of a lot of people.

Just as I did before, and just as I will always do, I must thank God, because without him, nothing is possible. Mom and Dad, thanks for listening to me drone on and on about a novel that I refused to let you read. Sharene and Bob, thank you for your guidance early in my career. WOWWS (Del and Paula), Julie, Brian, April, Frances, Lani, Cynthia B., Karl, and Manuel, thanks for all the support, critiques, and advice.

To the Wonderful Cynthia Leitich Smith (and yes, that should be your official name), you are a true champion of both YA literature and YA authors. I've always believed that mentors should be old and wrinkly and should walk around with a cane. You have none of those attributes, yet you are a great mentor, nevertheless.

Sara Crowe, thank you for finding my baby a good home (and thanks for the cookies). No author could ask for a better agent. Esther Hershenhorn, thank you for helping me make this novel all that it could be.

To Super Cool Editor Guy Andrew Karre, Editor Rhiannon Ross, and the folks at Flux, thank you for taking a chance on me. Your patience and dedication is what made this novel what it is today.

Thanks to the following centers and websites for an abundance of information: Austin Woman's Health Center (especially Leah), Atlanta Surgicenter, Planned Parenthood, the Guttmacher Institute, and Wolfram Mathworld.

And to Crystal, thanks for all of the above, times two. You will always be my rhombus.

Also by Varian Johnson

Red Polka Dot In A World Full of Plaid

"There are two ways to do great mathematics. The first is to be smarter than everybody else. The second way is to be stupider than everybody else—but persistent."

—*Raoul Bott*

Questions They Never Ask on the SAT

A very smart, attention-starved freshman (subject X) falls for the most popular guy in her class (subject Y). If X and Y date for at least three months, which of the following extra-curricular activities is X most likely to be involved in?

A: Backseat anatomy lessons, clothing optional.

B: Accuracy and precision experiments involving peeing onto a little plastic stick.

C: Two-hour biology lectures from a very disappointed father.

D: Field trips across state lines for "routine" medical procedures.

E: Proving the statistical fallacy of the statement, "It can't happen to me."

Note: More than one answer may apply.

chapter[1]
the shape of things 2(come)

I don't tutor high school students.

That was what I told Bryce when I started working at the West Columbia Community Center two and a half years ago. Maybe what I should have said was: *I don't tutor high school students, especially spoiled, superficial, popular high school students.*

Despite my decree, here stood Sarah Gamble, junior class goddess. She towered over me like she expected me to bow at her feet. It would have been one thing if she had walked up to me at school, but what was someone like her doing here?

"Hey, Rhonda," she said, like we were long-lost best friends. "You're just the person I was looking for."

She slid into the chair across from me. I couldn't help but notice how clean and smooth her cinnamon-toned skin was—it was like she paid acne to stay away from her face. Her smile was so large, I could count all thirty-two of her perfectly white teeth.

"I hear you're a pretty good tutor," she said as she twisted a strand of hair around her finger. "I need a little help with my trig homework."

I narrowed my eyes. "Nothing personal, but I don't usually tutor girls like you."

Sarah stopped smiling. *Finally.*

"And just what the hell does that mean?" She crossed her arms and stared me down.

I straightened my glasses. "There must be a mistake. The college students tutor high school students." I jerked my head toward the corner, where a group of college freshmen were dozing off.

"All I know is, my father donates a lot of money to this place." She pulled a textbook from her bag. "If you have a problem tutoring me, take it up with the bald guy with the bow tie. He sent me over here."

God, I hated uppity, popular girls like Sarah Gamble. The entire world had to revolve around them. (Of course, I used to be an uppity, popular girl myself, but that was another story.) Although I was a senior and she was a junior,

I saw enough of Sarah and her clique at school to know that I wanted nothing to do with her.

"I'll be back in a second," I said. I was layered in a turtleneck, sweater, and blue jeans, but I still felt like a naked whale in front of her. Even though she was wearing a heavy wool coat, I could imagine her rail-thin waist hiding underneath. I also had a skinny waist—it just happened to be hibernating below a lot of extra fat.

I marched to Bryce's office and pounded on the door. I didn't bother waiting for an invitation—I just barged in.

"You know I don't do high school students." I immediately thought about my choice of words and tried not to wince.

Bryce Mitchell, the director of the tutoring program, glanced up from his pile of paperwork. His bow tie looked like a miniature propeller on his huge body. "Don't yell. You'll disturb the students," he said in his schoolteacher voice.

I looked through his window. Sure enough, a roomful of brown faces stared back at me.

I shut his door. "Prep students are too bossy. They don't want to learn—they only want answers." I crossed my arms. "And isn't it against the rules for a high school student to tutor another high school student?"

"You made up that rule."

"Well, it's a good rule. It deserved to be made."

"You're tutoring her, end of story," Bryce said.

"But—"

"Do you know who that girl is?"

I stole a glance at the wannabe supermodel at my table. "Of course I do," I said. "What's she doing here, anyway? Girls like Sarah Gamble don't come here."

Bryce chuckled. "What do you mean by that? You're a black prep school student, just like her."

"Yeah, but I'm not a rich, stuck-up, black prep school student. That makes all the difference."

"Do y'all have classes together?"

I shook my head. "I only see her during lunch period. Sarah and the other divas put on a pretty good fashion show for the rest of us lowlifes."

Bryce ran his fingers over his non-existent hair. "She's also Deborah Gamble's daughter."

"I don't care if she's the Pope's daughter—I'm not tutoring her."

"Deborah Gamble sits on the South Carolina Supreme Court."

"I *am* an honor student," I said. "I know who Justice Gamble is." I puffed up my chest. "You think just because she's some big-shot judge that I'm gonna change my mind?"

He shot me a crocodile-toothed smile. "Did you know she got her undergraduate degree at Georgia Tech?"

Instantly, my chest deflated. "Georgia Tech?"

"Rhonda, Sarah Gamble needs help, and you're the best tutor I have. And while that's usually enough for you to tutor someone, I figured it wouldn't hurt your chances of getting a scholarship from Georgia Tech if you tutored the daughter of one of the school's most prestigious alumni." Bryce straightened his bow tie. "I'm sure a recommendation from Justice Gamble would carry a lot of weight."

I grabbed a tissue from Bryce's desk and began wiping my glasses. Sometimes I hated Bryce just as much as I hated the popular clique at school. I wanted to blow him off and tell him I had my integrity.

I slid my glasses back onto my nose. "Okay, I'll do it," I mumbled.

But then again, who needed integrity with a scholarship from the Georgia Institute of Technology?

I trudged back to the table. Sarah slaved away at an erasure-filled sheet of paper, the gold bracelet on her wrist clanking against the wooden table as she wrote. She was working so hard on her math problem, I wasn't sure if she even noticed when I walked up behind her and peeked over her shoulder.

"Maybe I can help," I said. I hated to see one of my students agonizing so much, even if I thought she was a snob.

Sarah glared at me. "So I guess you tutor girls like me now."

I took a deep breath. *Georgia Tech. Georgia Tech.*

"Sorry about that," I said. "I just wanted to make sure Bryce didn't get things mixed up."

She gave a half nod and turned back to her problem.

"Are you cold?" I asked, once I noticed she still had on her coat. "Do you want me to hang up your coat?"

"I'm fine," she snapped.

I sighed again. Maybe community college wasn't so bad after all.

"Why don't you walk me through your problem? Maybe I can help you find your mistake." As I sat down, I tried to ignore the loud creaking sound that the chair made.

I expected Sarah to throw a major hissy fit and complain about how the math was too hard, or how it was so unfair for her to be studying, or some crap like that, but she didn't. She just brushed her hair from her face, grabbed a new sheet of paper, and began the problem again.

"There's your mistake." I stabbed the sheet. "You can't use this trig formula here. Try using the tangent function."

Sarah stared at me like I had asked her to triple-integrate a fifth-order polynomial. "That *is* the tangent function, isn't it?"

My mouth dropped open. Today was going to be a *long* day.

I pulled my chair closer and began to work with her. I actually felt sorry for the girl. It seemed as if she had either missed weeks of class or she just didn't care for math at all. Eventually, we had to stop working on the current assignment and go three chapters back to re-cover material. Sarah and I were working so hard, I didn't realize the time until Bryce came over and tapped me on the shoulder.

"It's closing time," he said. "Wrap it up."

I glanced at my watch and turned to Sarah. "I didn't

realize how late it was. I'm sorry we couldn't get further along on your homework."

"Maybe if I hadn't spent so much time asking stupid questions..."

"That's what you're supposed to do, remember?" For the first time that night, I smiled. "And believe me, your questions weren't stupid. You should hear what some of my fourth graders ask me."

As much as it pained me to admit it, there was more to Sarah Gamble than her trendy, knee-high black boots and designer jeans. It wasn't like I had suddenly joined the Sarah Gamble Fan Club, but I did respect her a lot more after tutoring her. She was inquisitive, and she seemed like she really wanted to learn the material. That is, she seemed like she really wanted to learn the material while she was sitting at the table. Over the course of the hour, she took three extended trips to the bathroom. Each time she returned to the table, she was chewing on a thick wad of cherry-flavored gum.

I hoped she wasn't in the bathroom puking her brains out. (When I was the aforementioned popular girl, I'd had a few run-ins with vodka. But again, that was another story.) She was too coherent to be drunk. Knowing my luck, she was either anorexic or bulimic. It seemed as if girls like her were always either starving themselves or throwing up their tofu lunch. Maybe she needed a guidance counselor instead of a math tutor.

"If you continue to study the old material, you may be

able to catch up with the rest of the class in a few weeks." I zipped up my bookbag. "When's your next test?"

"Tomorrow."

I frowned. "You're kidding, right?"

"Don't worry. I've bombed plenty of tests—one more won't hurt."

I shook my head. "Not to pry, but what have you been doing for the past few months? You're not failing because you're dumb. You're failing because you don't have a solid background in trigonometry." I hoisted my bookbag onto my shoulder. "Who's your teacher?"

"Mr. Carey," she said. "At least it used to be Mr. Carey, until Mom yanked me out of his class."

I nodded. Mr. Carey's idea of an adequate math education was letting his students play poker in order to learn about probability.

"Mrs. Hawthorne is my new teacher. She's who suggested you."

Sarah and I walked out of the building and into the crisp, frigid air. Even though this was the South, Columbia still got pretty chilly in December.

"Thanks for helping me with my homework," Sarah said. Maybe the wind breezing through my ears caused me to hear incorrectly, but she actually sounded sincere.

"It's nothing," I said. "I'm just doing my job."

"I know it's your job, but I don't have to make it hard on you. I didn't mean to be so snappy back there." She winked. "The asshole disease runs in my family."

I couldn't help but laugh. However, I knew if my best friend, Gail, saw me chatting it up with Sarah like old pals, she'd burn me at the stake.

I followed Sarah into the parking lot. It didn't take a genius to figure out the sleek, navy blue Mercedes coupe was hers.

"I'm usually not mean," she said. "I just hate being forced to do anything." Sarah pulled her keys from her purse and unlocked her car door. "My mother can be a real bitch sometimes. I'd give anything to live with my father instead of her."

At least she *had* a mother to boss her around. I almost told her so, but I was just her tutor. It wasn't my place to say such things.

"Don't get me wrong, I like school and all," she continued. "But there are some things more important than trig."

That was easy for her to say. In my universe, there wasn't anything more important than grades. I didn't have the luxury or the desire to treat high school like an extended vacation. Good grades were the best way for me to escape this hellhole.

"Listen, most of the students that come here don't have the money to hire a private tutor," I said. "You do. You should think about getting one."

"Like I said before, it wasn't my idea to come."

"Well, did you think about getting someone at school to tutor you, instead of driving all the way out here?"

She looked down and dragged her feet along the

crumbling asphalt pavement. "Mom doesn't want anyone to know I'm getting tutored."

"There's nothing wrong with needing a tutor."

"Tell *her* that." Sarah readjusted her bag on her shoulder. "Listen, I appreciate all the help. I'll let you know how bad I failed when I come back."

Before I could reply, she had slipped into her car and slammed the door shut.

Well, at least she was coming back. The question was, was that good or bad?

∴

I unlocked the door and stepped into the kitchen. Dad was at the counter, surrounded by bags full of vegetables. A cloud of thick, black smoke hovered over one of the pans on the stove. His sweater was covered in flour, and the air was saturated with the aroma of raw onion and burnt chicken.

I sat my bookbag on the table. "Do you know what you're doing?"

Dad began to chop up an extremely withered-looking stalk of celery. "Jackie suggested I try out this recipe." He paused as he picked up a scrap of paper and held it in front of his face. "Orange Chicken. It's supposed to be low-fat."

I shook my head. In the seven years since Mom had died, Dad's interaction with the stove had been limited to boiling water and heating up leftovers. But now that he was dating, he had suddenly become a gourmet chef.

I didn't waste time looking in the pot—I picked up the phone and speed-dialed the pizza place. While I placed my order, I began to flip through the stack of mail on the table.

"Don't bother looking," Dad said, fanning smoke away from his face. "Not unless you want to pay the cable and electric bills."

I finished placing my order and hung up the phone. "Nothing from Georgia Tech?"

"Afraid not."

I had already been accepted to Clemson and the University of South Carolina. USC had even offered me a full scholarship. But—not to sound ungrateful—I couldn't care less. The only school that mattered to me was Georgia Tech. I had applied for one of Tech's most competitive (and lucrative) scholarships—the finalists were to be announced before the end of the year.

"Don't worry," Dad said, in his *Father Knows Best* tone of voice. "It'll come. Your math scores are too good for you not to get a scholarship."

Samuel Lee, my father, was a city engineer—or as he liked to call himself, "the best damn underpaid, overworked civil servant Columbia had ever seen." In addition to my passion for math and science, I also inherited my beautiful smile, light brown eyes, and rich cocoa skin from him. Unfortunately, he also passed along his nearsightedness, sausage-shaped fingers, and soft, pudgy mid-section.

Dad banged a spoon against the pan, trying to loosen a brown glob from it. "How was tutoring?"

"Interesting," I said. "I ended up tutoring a classmate from Piedmont."

Creases shot across his forehead. "When did *you* start tutoring high school kids?"

His question would have seemed innocent enough to the untrained observer, but I could already hear the worry in his voice. The frown on his face was as large as his pot-belly. He stuck a spoonful of his experimental goop in his mouth. Still frowning, he forced it down.

"Today was the first," I said. "Mrs. Hawthorne recommended me to one of her students. A junior." I paused and watched the steam begin to build in Dad's head. Time to release the pressure. "*She* needed help in trigonometry."

A weary smile came to his face. "That's great. I'm sure it's nice to teach something other than multiplication tables and simple arithmetic." He finally gave up on his experiment and turned off the stove. "You said she went to Piedmont, right? What's her name?"

"Sarah Gamble." I felt like I was in elementary school as I bounced over to him. "And her mother is Justice Deborah Gamble. Bryce thinks that if things go well, she'll offer to write me a recommendation if I get selected as a finalist for the President's Achievement Program."

By now, Dad was beaming. "With your test scores and

a letter from Justice Gamble, you'd almost be guaranteed a scholarship." He quickly stifled his smile. "Of course, we don't need to expect anything out of this. And even if you don't get a scholarship to Georgia Tech, as long as you get accepted, I can pay for it." He peered down at me. "That's what fathers are supposed to do."

I felt my face sour. "You don't have to worry about paying for me to go to college. I'll get the scholarship."

"I'm sure you will, Rhonda. I was just saying that if things don't work out—"

"I'll get the scholarship," I said, crossing my arms over my chest.

We stared at each other in silence for a few seconds. The black smoke that had been floating over the stove suddenly seemed to have surrounded us. I thought about apologizing for being so short with him, but decided against it. It was easier for both of us if I just kept quiet.

Dad sighed. "Why don't you tell me about your new student?"

I nodded, happy to be crossing back into neutral territory. "Sarah seems nice," I said. "She's one of the most popular girls at school. She's a cheerleader and president of the…"

My voice trailed off as a familiar grimace came to Dad's face. His eyes narrowed and his jaw turned into concrete.

"Honey, you've got to watch out for girls like her. They can be a handful."

I shook my head. So much for neutral territory.

"Maybe you shouldn't tutor her. You know, so you're not…tempted to fall back into your old crowd. You don't really need a recommendation from Justice Gamble. Your grades are good enough to speak for themselves."

He stepped toward me. I thought he was going to hug me, but instead he reached into his pocket, pulled out some cash, and dropped it on the counter. "Call me when the pizza gets here. I'm going to my room to watch a little of the basketball game."

I pretended to count the money as Dad strode off, but as soon as I heard the familiar click of his bedroom door shutting, I dropped the cash and made a beeline to the freezer. By the time the pizza arrived twenty minutes later, I had eaten two bowls of strawberry ice cream, both smothered in chocolate syrup and topped with sprinkles.

There was no doubt about it—tomorrow was definitely shaping up to be another day for the elastic waistband pants.

Advanced Calculus Studies—Class Breakdown

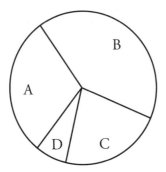

Group A: The Doodlers (Who says art and math can't mix?) (5 students)

Group B: The Techno Geeks (They spend most of the class period dreaming about their Internet girlfriends.) (8 students)

Group C: The Efficiency Experts (Why sit in a boring class and do nothing when you can be working on another teacher's assignments?) (3 students)

Group D: The Curve-Busters (The only ones that seem to give a damn about a useless class.) (1 student)

chapter^2
common(denominators)

For fifty-two minutes and forty-nine seconds, I stared at the back of Gail's head as she fired question after question at our teacher. Mr. Miller probably lost two gallons of water a day from all the sweating he did in our class.

Not that the rest of us cared. We had already passed all the math-related Advanced Placement classes we were allowed to take in high school. This class was basically a glorified study hall—well, for everyone except Gail.

As soon as the bell rang, the entire class sighed in relief and began collecting their bags.

I balled up a piece of paper and threw it at Gail's head. "Do you have to ask so many questions?"

Gail twisted around in her desk. "With as much as my parents are shelling out for my education, I feel I can ask as many questions as I want."

"But Gail, you already know the answers to most of the questions. Hell, you know the material better than Mr. Miller."

"We *all* know the material better than Mr. Miller."

I rose from my desk. "Still, you shouldn't show off. You may need him to write a recommendation—"

"Speaking of recommendations," Gail began, as she leapt from her desk and grabbed my wrist, "guess what I got in the mail yesterday."

I could already tell by the sound of her voice. "Stanford?"

She nodded so hard, I thought she was going to shake her teeth loose. "I got in," she said.

"Don't tell me you're surprised. You got a perfect math score on the SAT."

"Now that you mention it…"

I rolled my eyes. "I would hate you, if you weren't my best friend."

She laughed. "I'm just happy that it's over with. I feel like I've aged ten years over the past three months."

"Don't be so smug. Some of us are still aging, remember."

Gail and I walked out of the classroom and down the

hallway. "I guess you haven't heard anything from Georgia Tech," she said, her voice a little less cheerful. "Well, if it makes you feel better, my sister didn't find out about her scholarship until after Christmas. And if she got a scholarship, you'll definitely get one."

Gail Smith had been my best friend since I met her on the first day of tenth grade, her first year at Piedmont Academy. I always joked that she had a plain name, but her looks certainly weren't plain. She was part Korean, part Cuban, and part African. Her skin was a striking bronze, her hair was a reddish-brown mix. And not only was she pretty, but she could recite π to the fortieth decimal place.

We went through the lunch line and headed to our usual table, way off in the corner of the cafeteria. The last of my merry band of super-smart outcasts, Xavier, was already sitting, his fingers punching away at the keys on his laptop. Xavier was the editor of our school newspaper, but being that he only had a staff of two, he ended up writing most of the articles himself.

We slid into our seats, and Gail quickly informed Xavier of her good news. Xavier slumped farther in his seat and looked at me. "So I guess that means it'll just be me and you taking the SAT this Saturday," he said.

"I've taken the SAT four times, and I still can't get my Verbal scores up." I bit into a soggy carrot stick. "I think I'm stuck with the scores I have."

"At least you have the full ride from USC to fall back on," Xavier said.

"USC isn't an option."

Gail and Xavier exchanged looks, but didn't say anything. They just didn't understand—I couldn't stay in Columbia and go to USC. I *had* to escape. I needed a fresh start.

I began to pull out my chemistry book, but stopped once I caught a glimpse of Sarah Gamble. She and the rest of the cheerleaders had set up shop at a table in the middle of the cafeteria. They wore the same drab blue blazers as everyone else, but somehow they made them look like fashion statements. The way she laughed and carried on, she didn't look like a girl that had failed a major test today.

"Maybe she passed after all," I mumbled to myself.

"Maybe who passed?" Xavier boomed. Xavier was short and skinny, with spiky blonde hair and a voice like a cannon. Every time he spoke, his Adam's apple expanded so much, I thought he was choking.

I snapped my head toward him. "No one," I said, a little too quickly.

That caught Gail's interest. She pushed her tray away and scooted closer to me. "You're mighty jumpy."

I slid away from her. "Everybody'll think I'm gay if we sit this close to each other."

"Come on, Rhonda," she said. "They probably think that anyway."

Good point.

"What's his name?" Gail asked.

"Who?" I replied.

She shook her head. "We can spend all day playing this cat-and-mouse game, or you can save both of us some time and tell me his name."

I sighed and readjusted my glasses. "I wish I *were* thinking about a guy. Y'all know I don't have any type of love life."

They both nodded and went back to eating their lunch, and I immediately wanted to throw my tray at them. I hated that they conceded defeat so quickly. What if I *had* been thinking about a guy? Just because I hadn't gone out on a date in almost three years didn't mean I couldn't.

Out of the three of us, Gail's love life was in the best shape. Her boyfriend, a freshman at MIT, was as exciting as a brown paper bag, but at least he treated her nicely. My love life was ground zero right now—though at least the rubble proved I had once *had* a love life, unlike Xavier. Xavier was a career virgin trying to find a new line of work.

Of course, none of our love lives compared to Sarah's. Girls like her could—

"Rhonda, what are you looking at?" Xavier asked.

I quickly turned back to the group. I hadn't realized I was staring at Sarah again.

"Okay, what's really going on?" Gail asked. "I know you're up to something."

"Don't bother answering," Xavier said. "I see exactly what you were looking at."

Everyone at the table turned and glanced in the direction that I had been staring. Sarah was standing up now, talking to her older brother, David.

"You were staring at David Gamble, weren't you?" Gail demanded. "Don't tell me you have a crush on him."

I tugged at my collar. "Of course I don't."

"What's wrong with David?" Xavier asked. "He's in my biology class. He seems really nice."

"And that makes you an expert on David Gamble?" Gail folded her arms across her chest. "Rhonda doesn't need a boyfriend like him, anyway. Especially since in less than a year, she'll be a freshman at Georgia Tech."

Xavier sat up in his seat. "But *you* have a boyfriend—"

"Lewis isn't like these immature boys we go to school with." Gail's voice dropped a little as she turned toward me. "And anyway, my situation is entirely different than Rhonda's."

I frowned, but didn't say anything. What could I say? Gail was exactly right.

"I'm not saying that Rhonda shouldn't have a boyfriend," she continued. "I'm saying that she shouldn't have a boyfriend like *him*."

"Why are we having this conversation?" I shook my head. "I wasn't even looking at David Gamble."

"Then who were you looking at?" Gail asked.

My stomach began to churn. "Um…"

"You were staring pretty hard in that direction," Xavier

said. There was a slight glint in his eye. "Do you have a crush on his sister?"

"Shut up, Xavier," both Gail and I said.

Gail sighed. "Do I have to remind you that he plays on the basketball team? With Christopher?"

Xavier nodded. "Christopher *is* a jerk."

"How many times do I have to say that I'm not interested in David Gamble?" I paused and glared at Xavier. "Or his sister." I stood and grabbed my tray. "I think I'm done with lunch for today."

I tossed my half-eaten ham sandwich in the trash and marched to the library. But as I walked there, I realized I wasn't mad at Gail and Xavier because they didn't think I could get a guy like David Gamble. I was mad because *I* knew I couldn't get a guy like David. And that wouldn't have been so bad, except that I really *did* have a crush on him.

David and Sarah had transferred to Piedmont Academy last year. They didn't have any trouble fitting in with the rich crowd. Most of the people around here didn't see things in terms of race. Green was the preferred color of choice.

Sarah was an instant hit with everyone at school. I had heard her name mentioned by four different guys before I even caught a glimpse of the girl. Finally, at the end of the day, I saw her. She was tall and lanky, like a supermodel, with full red lips and perfectly shaped hazel eyes. She was the most beautiful person I had ever seen.

I hated her instantly.

David was a much more rugged version of his sister. He, too, was tall and lanky, but that was about the only similarity between them. It always seemed that Sarah was the center of attention, while David shied away from the crowd. The only reasons he was popular was because he was Sarah's brother, he dated popular girls, and he was a basketball player. He was also extremely cute, but he never smiled, which I couldn't understand. I even had a class with him last semester. On the first day of Spanish class, in the process of rushing into the room, I damn near ran him over. But instead of being angry, David just apologized in that deep, hypnotizing voice of his and allowed me to walk in first.

And even though I knew I would never date him, I couldn't deny that my heart fluttered, if only for a thousandth of a second.

∴

"How did you do on your test?" I asked as Sarah slammed her books on the table the following evening.

The look on her face said it all.

"How bad?"

"Pretty damn bad."

I motioned for her to sit next to me. "We just need to work a little harder."

She shook her head. "I'm through with this tutoring bullshit. I'll take the class over again in the summer."

"But what about your mother?"

"Fuck her," she said, her voice carrying across the room. "I don't care anymore."

I sat back in my chair and glanced toward Bryce's office. He was already headed toward our table.

"Maybe we should go for a walk or something," I said.

Her face seemed to relax at that thought. She chewed on her lip for a second before nodding. "But what about your elementary school kids?"

"Most of my regulars were already in. Bryce has rearranged my schedule so I'll have about thirty minutes every other day to tutor you."

"Tell him to change it back."

Bryce reached the table. "Is there a problem?"

"No problem," I said, already standing. "We're just going for a walk."

He flashed me a fatherly look. "I don't know...it'll be dark soon."

"Don't worry, we'll be right outside." I grabbed Sarah by the arm and dragged her out of the building before Bryce could say anything else.

Sarah pulled her hair from her face and rubbed her eyes. Her black mascara was beginning to smear across her cheeks. She would have made a beautiful raccoon.

"It's just that I felt so good after you helped me." She plopped down on the curb and twirled her hair around her fingers. "I even studied for a few extra hours after I left the center. When I walked into that classroom, I knew I was going to pass that test."

"What happened?"

"I was too slow. I was only able to finish half the test."

"You'll get it next time," I said. "You've got to keep plugging away at it."

Sarah looked at me and opened her mouth as if she was going to say something. But instead, she leapt from the curb and ran to the bushes. Seconds later, she was throwing up.

I jumped up and ran to her. By the time I got there, she had finished "fertilizing" the shrubbery. She spat a few times and wiped her mouth with the back of her hand. "Stomach virus," she mumbled.

I took a quick sniff of her as she passed by. She didn't smell like alcohol, unless she was taking shots of peach-scented perfume.

"You know what I need?" she said. "A pint of ice cream."

"But you just threw up."

Sarah smirked. "Can you think of a better way for me to get this nasty taste out of my mouth?" She headed toward a convenience store across the street. "I only hope they have French vanilla."

I smiled and followed her. I guess even a snob had to have some good points.

.˙.

"Why are you staring at me like that?" Sarah asked. We sat at the bus stop around the corner from the center. I could imagine how crazy we looked, eating ice cream outside in the first week of December. No wonder the bus didn't bother stopping as it passed by.

"I'm not staring at you." I popped the last of my ice cream sandwich into my mouth and crumpled the paper wrapper in my fist. "I just don't want you to give up, okay? You're really smart, whether you believe it or not."

"Why do you care?"

I shrugged. "I'm your tutor. It's part of the job."

"So this is strictly a business relationship." Sarah sighed. "At least you're being honest."

I shook my head. "I don't mean to be rude. I just don't usually hang out with girls like you. No offense, but we don't have enough in common to be friends."

"Other than eating ice cream in December?"

I smiled. "Yeah, other than that."

Sarah finished her ice cream and stuffed her hands into her oversized coat. For someone that was so fashion savvy, I didn't know why she was wearing a coat that was obviously too big for her.

"You feeling any better?" I asked. "You don't need to throw up again, do you?"

She gave off a forced, spotty laugh. "I'm okay," she said, looking away from me. "I'll be glad when I get over this virus."

"How long have you been sick?"

She fidgeted in her seat. "I don't know. Maybe a few weeks."

"A few weeks? What type of stomach virus lasts that long?"

Sarah didn't reply. The color in her face had disappeared—I was afraid she was going to vomit again. She had the worst virus I had ever seen. For as much as she was throwing up, it was almost like she was—

My mouth dropped open, and suddenly, *I knew.* Unfortunately for Sarah, everything now made sense.

I toyed with the buttons on my coat, trying to decide if I was going to say anything or not. I slowly exhaled, watching the white fog escape from my lips and disappear into the night.

"How far along are you?" I finally asked.

Sarah whipped her head around and looked at me like a deer in headlights. "What…what are you talking about?"

I inched closer to her. "The bulky clothes and the vomiting gave you away."

Sarah's entire body drooped. "Seven weeks," she said under her breath. It was the first time I had ever heard her speak quietly.

"Does anyone else know?"

She shook her head. "I don't even know why I wear the bulky clothes. I haven't gained a pound in the past two months, but every time I look in the mirror, I feel like my stomach is getting bigger."

I flashed back to the earlier scene of Sarah throwing up. "How bad is your morning sickness?" I asked.

"Pretty bad," she said. "Mine just doesn't come in the morning, though. It seems like I'm always throwing up."

I closed my eyes and went through a mental checklist. "Have you tried crackers? Or maybe mints?"

"Doesn't work."

"Then try ginger. You can take it as a tea or as tablets."

She nodded. "That's exactly what I read on the Internet." She struggled to get up from her sitting position on the bench before frowning at me. "Hey, wait a minute. How do you know that?"

As I looked at Sarah, a million explanations (okay, lies) popped into my head. I mean, she was just my student, I was just her tutor, right? I wasn't obligated to share my life history with her.

But as much as I wanted to, I couldn't lie to her. I knew how miserable she felt. I had felt the same way.

I coughed a few times to try to clear my throat. I had to force myself to open my mouth. Secrets like mine didn't offer themselves up without a fight.

"My doctor suggested the same thing a few years ago," I said.

I stared at Sarah, as her gaze transformed from a look of questioning to a look of shock to a final look of understanding.

"Maybe we have more than a love for ice cream in common after all," I said.

Sarah nodded. "Maybe so."

I rose from the bench, and Sarah and I headed back

to the center. We didn't speak a single word on the walk back. There wasn't much to talk about. By the time we got to the community center, the tutoring session was over. We ran inside to get our books.

"Are you coming back?" I asked.

"Maybe."

"You know, Mrs. Hawthorne is a pretty fair teacher. You may be able to convince her to give you a re-test."

"I'll think about it," she said.

I yanked a sheet of paper out of my notebook and scribbled my number on it. "If you end up studying this weekend, feel free to give me a call."

Sarah folded the notebook paper into crisp, neat lines and tucked it into her purse. "If I have some questions on…other stuff, can I give you a call?"

"Any time."

Sarah gave me a quick smile before turning and waltzing out the door. I sighed and followed her out. Whether she realized it or not, Sarah Gamble was just beginning her own "Year of Hell." I only hoped it would go better for her than it did for me.

chapter³
redefining(Rhonda)

My own "Year of Hell" didn't start off terribly badly. I was a freshman at Piedmont Academy, one of the premiere private high schools in Columbia. I hated the stuck-up atmosphere of the school, but Piedmont's math and science departments were the best in the city. If I wanted to go to a top-notch engineering school, this was the only place to be.

On the first day of class, I met Christopher McCullough, a half-white, half-black preacher's son with a ferocious dunk. Within a month, I was his algebra tutor. By Thanksgiving, I was his girlfriend. He was perfect, and for the first time since Mom died, I felt important. Special. Loved.

I made my first mistake when I had sex with him. I wished I could say it was romantic or spectacular or even enjoyable. But all I remembered was that it was in the back of his mother's Saab, it hurt like hell, and it lasted all of forty-five seconds.

The second mistake I made was that I kept on sleeping with him. It got so extreme, we would sneak off during lunch for quickies (and let me stress the *quick* portion of the word). I really hated sleeping with him, but I thought I loved him. His affection more than made up for the few minutes of sexual discomfort.

But then, it all ended. Christopher showed up one day and dumped me. He didn't even wait until after school— he did it during lunch. He said some crap about needing space, but apparently he didn't need *that* much space, being that he had a new girlfriend by the following week.

After Christopher dumped me, things were never the same between me and my other so-called friends. They would do things like plan events and mysteriously forget to invite me. Truthfully, I wasn't surprised when I showed up for lunch one day and found someone had taken my usual seat.

So there I was, lonely and depressed. I didn't have a boyfriend. I didn't have any other friends. And when I thought it couldn't get any worse, it happened: I missed my period.

By this time, Christopher had transformed from my knight in shining armor into the shallow, uncaring, spineless loser that he really was. He had the audacity to claim it wasn't his. He didn't even have the decency to face Dad when I told him.

Dad was the one that signed the consent forms at the women's clinic. He waited with me in the lobby with all the other young, scared, confused girls. He waved goodbye to me as the nurse ushered me into the cold room for the procedure. He was the one that helped me to the car when it was over, and fed me soup when I could finally eat again. He was there when I magically transformed from his baby girl into his great disappointment.

After the procedure, I rededicated myself to my studies. I found comfort in the exactness of math and the precision of science. And like Euclid, the father of geometry, did in the *Elements*, I even created a set of rules that would govern the remaining three years of life in high school.

Rhonda's Elements

Postulate 1: Boys are not to be trusted.

Postulate 2: I am not to be trusted around boys.

Postulate 3: Popular, spoiled, stuck-up, superficial people should be avoided at all times.

Postulate 4: My studies are the most important thing in my life.

From these postulates, I created the twenty-one theorems that now shaped my life. My theorems ranged from the flippant (Theorem 18 proved that cake and ice cream should be part of my daily required food intake), to the serious (Theorem 4 proved that I could achieve extreme happiness by earning a scholarship to Georgia Tech).

My rules may have seemed a little extreme to most people, but I didn't care. I'd take my Elements over the Year of Hell any day.

∴

"How are things going with the Gamble girl?" Dad asked as we sat at the table. Tonight was spaghetti night, and Dad was already on his second helping.

I shook some Parmesan cheese over my food. *Oh, pretty bad. She's seven weeks pregnant and too scared to tell anyone. But other than that, she's great.* "It's okay," I said. "She's a nice girl."

"I think I remember seeing her at one of the football games. She's very pretty, although it looked like she wore too much makeup for someone her age." He spun his fork between his fingers, collecting a large amount of noodles on the end. "You know, your mother never wore makeup. She didn't need it."

Dad was right, Mom was beautiful. No, better yet, she was perfect. She was the type of mother that baked cookies and sewed Halloween costumes. She had eyes that could illuminate the scariest of dark bedrooms. She had a smile that made you feel all warm and toasty on the inside.

"Do you have any plans this weekend?" he asked.

I shook my head. "Maybe we can still get tickets to the

USC game." I pushed a meatball around with my fork. "It's been a really long time since we've gone to a game together."

When I was growing up, we always went to the college games. We'd even go to a few professional games in Charlotte. But all of that stopped after my freshman year. It was like there was some unspoken punishment I had been on ever since then. Now the closest we got to attending sporting events together was watching highlights on the evening news.

Dad was too busy stuffing food down this throat to look up. "Sorry, honey. Jackie and I are going out this weekend."

I rolled my eyes. "The Teeny Bopper."

Jackie, Dad's new girlfriend, was about as sophisticated and graceful as a bucket of spit. I didn't know what Dad saw in her—she didn't even compare to Mom.

"Don't you think you're robbing the cradle? You're old enough to be her father."

"Maybe if I had started having children when I was twelve." As he took a pause from his meal, the creases around his eyes deepened. "It's been almost seven years," he said, his voice low and quiet. "I had to start dating eventually."

I shrugged. "You're the one who still keeps Mom's picture on your nightstand, not me."

As soon as I said the words, I regretted them. Dad dropped his gaze to his plate and slowly chewed his food. I could see his jaw muscles tighten with every bite he took.

"I'm sorry," I said. "I didn't mean it like that. I'm glad you keep Mom's picture up."

He just nodded and continued to eat. I knew I should have done a better job of apologizing, but truthfully, I hated the idea of Dad dating Jackie. She wasn't Mom. She had no right coming in here and trying to be Mom. Dad and I had made it this long on our own. We didn't need anyone swooping in now.

Thankfully, the phone rang, making us both jump. Usually, we had a rule that no one answered the phone until we finished dinner. But with the way both of us were feeling, I thought we needed a little break.

I leapt from the table and answered the phone on the second ring.

"This is Sarah Gamble. May I speak with Rhonda?"

Sarah's voice was confident and perky, the total opposite of what it sounded like earlier that evening. She sounded more like a cheerleader than a mother-to-be.

"Hold on for a second, okay?" I held my hand over the receiver and looked at Dad. "I'm gonna take this, okay?"

He nodded, and I ran off to my room with the cordless phone. I cranked up the radio and plopped down on the bed. "Hey, you sound much better," I said. "You were really stressed out earlier today."

"Yeah, it wasn't anything that a quick pedicure couldn't fix."

I looked down at my midsection. Maybe I should follow her lead and get pedicures instead of eating when I was depressed.

"Well, the cheerleading coach called tonight. Sure enough, I got kicked off the squad."

"Is that why you were getting tutored? So you could continue cheerleading?"

Sarah chuckled. "I couldn't care less about being a cheerleader. I didn't like standing out there at those football games and freezing my ass off, anyway. But Mom was a cheerleader, so I was destined to be a cheerleader as well. She said it builds character. The only thing it did for me was give me sore feet and a hoarse voice."

"Does this mean you're finished with tutoring?" I asked.

"No, but I am finished with going to the community center. Mom finally caved and decided to let me hire a tutor. I need more one-on-one help, and I just can't get it there."

I hated to agree, but Sarah was right. Bryce had rearranged my schedule so I could tutor Sarah, but realistically those thirty minutes every other day weren't enough. She was smart, but she had way too much material to make up in order to pass.

"Well, I know a few good private tutors." I grabbed my address book from my desk. "There are a few girls at USC that—"

"I don't want another tutor," she said. "I was hoping you could be my private tutor. You know, maybe you could come over to my place for a few hours a week and give me some extra help. I'd pay you, of course."

I stopped paging through my address book. "I don't think that would be a good idea."

"Why not?"

Um, let's see. My father thinks that if I spend too much time with you, I'll end up on all fours in an empty classroom with the next guy that approaches me. I am totally speechless when I'm around your brother. And I don't know if I can handle being this close to you, especially after learning about the "situation" growing inside your stomach. I've been down that road before, and I have no interest in going on the trip again, even if only as a backseat driver.

I grabbed a blanket and threw it over my toes. "I don't want to take time away from my studies."

"Come on," Sarah said. "You're a genius. You probably don't even need to study."

I shook my head. "I wish I could, but—"

"Listen, I'm sure you know who my mother is. She could be a big help when you start applying to colleges. Where are you thinking about going to school?"

The words were out of my mouth before I realized it. "Georgia Tech."

"That's perfect," she yelled, as if she were still a cheerleader. "My mother went to Tech."

I took a deep breath. "I know," I said. "I was kinda hoping she'd write me a recommendation…"

"You help me get my grades up, and the old hag will probably not only write you a recommendation, she'll hand-deliver you to the president of the college." There was a slight pause, and her voice reverted back to that of the scared girl at the bus stop. "I really need someone to talk to about my...predicament. You're the only friend I have that I can talk to about it."

I almost dropped the phone. Did she call me her friend? This week was the first time I had ever really spoken to the girl, and we were already best buddies?

Man, she must have really been hard up for someone to talk to.

By the time we got off the phone, Sarah had hired herself a private tutor. The way it was looking, she may have gotten a friend in the process, whether I wanted to be that friend or not.

chapter[4]
irrational(numbers)

I felt anxious as I stood at Sarah's doorstep, waiting for our first private tutoring session. I rang the doorbell, and then knocked twice on the sturdy wooden door for good measure. The house was an island in an ocean of green grass—it was almost a half-mile from the gated entrance to the front door. Stoic oak trees lined the perimeter of the grounds, guarding the house against unwelcome, prying eyes. The grounds themselves were immaculate—not one stray leaf from the oak trees littered the yard. Closer to the house sat perfectly square ficus hedges. The lawn was flawless, save for the few renegade wildflowers creeping up around the base of one of the shrubs. Apparently, even people like the Gambles had weed problems.

I turned my attention back to the door once I heard it open. I expected Sarah, or her mother, or even a maid to answer the door. Instead, I was greeted by one hundred and fifty pounds of cuteness.

"Hey, Rhonda," David said. "Come on in."

I could feel the heat rising to my face as I entered the house. God, what was wrong with me? Remember Postulate 1—*Boys are not to be trusted.*

David's eyes were hazel like Sarah's, but not quite as inviting. "Sarah's on the phone, but she should be off in a second."

I nodded quickly and flashed him a weak smile. Although his expression stayed the same, it seemed like his eyes relaxed, if just a little.

I followed David into the living room. The furniture could have been wrapped in cellophane, it seemed so new. A huge portrait of the Gamble family hung over the fireplace. The portrait was probably a few years old, but the children looked the same. Sarah was smiling and David was brooding.

"Why don't you have a seat," David said as he headed down the hallway. "I'll get Sarah."

I was almost afraid to sit down. The furniture looked extremely soft and comfortable. The last thing I wanted to do was leave a huge, permanent butt print in their designer sofa.

A few minutes later, Sarah burst into the room (unfortunately, David was nowhere to be seen). Sarah actually came up and hugged me. I was too stunned to hug her back.

"I'm glad you came," she said. "Let's get started."

I followed Sarah to the kitchen. Her books were strewn across the table, along with two platters of cookies.

"Our cook outdoes herself sometimes. Help yourself."

For the first time in my life, I was too nervous to eat. I pushed one of the platters away from the edge of the table and pulled out my calculator and notebook. "Did you talk to Mrs. Hawthorne about your grades?"

"Yeah, she said I could take another exam in a couple of weeks. If I show significant progress, she'll pass me."

"Then let's back up a few chapters. I think if we reinforce your background in trig, you'll do much better on your next test."

Nine problems, fifty-seven minutes, and one and a half cookie platters later (did you really expect me *not* to eat any of those cookies?), David walked into the room. Sarah didn't even look up from the table. I, on the other hand, had to fight to keep my gaze glued to Sarah's paper. My heart started beating even faster when I heard him approaching the table. He placed his hands on the back of my chair. I could feel his long, skinny fingers slightly graze my back. I swallowed hard, but still didn't look up.

"Use the cotangent function," he said as his voice flowed over my shoulder and spilled onto the table. "It'll make it simpler."

I studied Sarah's paper. David was right, to a degree.

"You could do that, Sarah," I said, pointing toward her paper. "But look at your problem more closely. See if you can cancel some of the terms in the denominator and numerator."

Sarah gasped. "Wait a minute, I can cancel this, and this, and this," she said, striking out terms with her pencil. "And then if I use this function..."

Sarah didn't have to finish explaining the problem. She had already seen the answer in her mind and now was letting her fingers catch up.

I finally glanced at David. I wasn't sure, but I thought I noticed a small grin on his face.

"Good job," he said, although I didn't know if he was talking to me or Sarah. "I'm taking the rest of the cookies."

He grabbed the remaining cookies and was out the door.

"Don't mind David," Sarah said after he left the room. "Sometimes he forgets he's only a year older than me. He thinks he knows everything."

"It sounds like he knows what he's talking about when it comes to trigonometry."

"Don't be fooled by the pretty jump shot," she said. "David is a closet nerd. He knows trig like I know fashion."

"Then why don't you get him to tutor you?"

"I tried doing that, but David is a horrible tutor. Instead of teaching me concepts, he just gave me the answers. That works fine when you're turning in homework, but unless

David was going to take my exams for me, it wouldn't have worked."

About twenty minutes later, David returned to the kitchen. He dropped the empty platter on the counter, but didn't rush out of the room. I could see him out of the corner of my eye, wiping away invisible crumbs from the stovetop.

"I don't think Mom will make it home in time for dinner," David said.

"Good," Sarah replied, without looking up from her book.

For a few seconds, the air in that room was as stale and stiff as a two-month-old loaf of bread. I looked at my hand and pretended my fingernails were the most interesting things in the world.

David sighed. "I'm going to order Chinese. Shrimp-fried rice okay?"

"Make sure you get a few extra packets of soy sauce," Sarah said, her pencil flying away on her paper.

David nodded, and I expected him to leave again. Instead, he looked at me. "Do you want anything?"

Sarah finally pulled her face from out of her book. "Didn't you hear me? I said—"

"I was talking to Rhonda, not you." David walked to the table and took a seat across from me. "This is me and Sarah's usual Saturday-night routine when we don't have any plans. We order Chinese food and watch bad action movies. You're welcome to stay—that is, unless you have other plans."

Sarah's eyes were as wide as the platters the cookies had been served on. She gave off a small chuckle. "Yeah, why don't you stay?"

I shook my head. "I'm sorry, but I have plans. I'm spending the night with my aunt."

"Too bad," David said. "Maybe next time."

I felt my mouth break into a smile. "Yeah, maybe so."

David rose from his seat, circled the table, and rustled Sarah's hair. Then he leaned over and planted a fat, wet, slobbery kiss on her forehead.

"Stop it," Sarah yelled. But as angry as she tried to sound, I could hear the laughter in her voice. "Just order the food, okay? Rhonda and I are almost done."

"Are you sure you don't want to stay?" he asked me, his eyes twinkling like Sarah's.

I wished more than anything that I could have cancelled my plans. I would have gladly stayed here with David (and Sarah, of course). But I had my own Saturday night plans to keep.

"Sorry, but I can't. Ask me again—maybe next time will be different."

He nodded one final time, and left the room.

I glanced at Sarah. Her head was tilted to the side, and she had a goofy grin on her face. "Did my brother just ask you out?"

"What?" It suddenly got very hot in the room. I took

off my glasses and wiped the lenses. "What makes you think that?"

"I have had countless people over here before, but you're the only person he has ever invited to stay for dinner." She leaned closer to me. "Plus, he's been asking a lot of questions about you."

"He has?" I asked, my voice a little too giddy. I shook off my excitement. "I'm sure it's nothing. He's just being friendly."

"Friendly, my ass." She let out a loud, bellowing laugh. "You have such a crush on him, don't you?"

My body temperature jumped up a few more degrees. "Of course not."

"Well, just between you and me, I think y'all would make a good couple. I'd rather see him with you than with those flaky chicks I hang out with at school. He needs a girl with some depth."

I began to laugh, but stopped when Sarah stood up. Maybe I was imagining it, but her jeans seemed tighter than usual.

Sarah must have realized I was looking at her stomach. "Is it noticeable?" she asked.

I shook my head. "Not yet."

She began closing her books. "I tried the ginger. It really does help a lot." She rubbed her stomach. "I must be the only girl that gets morning sickness in the afternoon."

"I was the same way," I said. "Have you decided what you're going to do yet?"

"No, not yet," she replied. "What did you do? Did you keep it?"

"No, I had—" I paused for a second, shaking my head. "No, I didn't keep it."

Once again, a stale feeling crept into the room. I hurriedly gathered my stuff. "So I'll see you next week, okay?" I said, my mouth going at full speed. I felt like I was going to catch on fire in there. I had to get out of that house.

"Okay," she said. "Hold on a second. Let me grab my coat and I'll walk you out."

"Don't worry about it," I said, already heading toward the door. "I can let myself out."

I wasn't sure if Sarah said anything after that—I was moving too fast to listen. My stomach had tightened into a huge knot. I felt like *I* was the one with morning sickness.

I bolted out of the house and ran to my car. It was only after I was safely strapped into the driver's seat that I stopped shaking.

Maybe morning sickness was contagious after all.

chapter[5]
solving4(x)

Helen Cassidy wasn't really my aunt, although you couldn't tell her otherwise. She was Mom's best friend from college, the yin to my mother's yang. Dad didn't care much for Helen, but he still encouraged me to spend time with her. He knew I needed some connection to Mom, and Helen was the best I had. My mother's parents had died when I was young, and she was an only child.

Helen's home was the total opposite of the Gamble house. The front yard—if you could call a few blades of grass and clumps of red clay a yard—was littered with leaves, cigarette butts, and whatever other trash the wind blew onto it. Her house was a simple two-bedroom structure with just enough room for her and her cats. More times than not, I pictured myself living in that very same house with those very same cats one day.

I unlocked the door and crept into the silent house. "Helen, are you home?"

The only answer I received was the purr of the fat, orange tabby sitting in the middle of the kitchen.

I threw my stuff on the table and made my way to the backyard. If she wasn't in the house, the only other place Helen could be was in her work shed. That was where she created all of her masterpieces.

Helen was an art teacher by day, a master sculptor by night. Every time I saw her, she was working on her "next big masterpiece"—the one that would make her rich and famous. The last time I was here, her big thing was miniature castles made from kitty litter. Unfortunately, she had to abandon that idea when one of the cats mistook Buckingham Palace for the bathroom.

Sure enough, Helen was in the little shack, sanding down a piece of wood. She looked up long enough to acknowledge my presence, before focusing her attention back on her task.

After spending a few more moments sanding down the wooden plank, she held it up. I could tell she had been sanding down the piece for a long time. Mountains of sawdust surrounded her. Helen blew a few remaining specks of sawdust off the plank, before promptly throwing the wood into the garbage.

"Why did you trash that wood?" I asked.

She pulled off her goggles and facemask, and brushed wisps of reddish-gray hair from her pale, freckled face. "Don't need the wood," she said. "I need the sawdust."

I didn't even want to ask what she was working on.

Helen grabbed a small brush and dustpan from her counter and swept up her precious sawdust. "How did it go over at Sarah's house?"

My mind went back to my hyperventilating episode in Sarah's driveway. I smoothed my plaid skirt over my thighs. "It was okay."

"Just okay?"

I nodded. "For a preppy girl, Sarah is very sweet. I really like tutoring her."

"Is she showing yet?"

I shook my head. Helen was the only person I had told Sarah's secret to. Helen did a great job of keeping my secrets, so I figured she could handle one more.

"Was anyone else over there? Her mother, perhaps?"

I felt hot again, but I didn't feel sick, like before. Now, it felt like my face was ablaze.

"No, just her."

Helen laughed. "I don't know who is a worse liar, you or your mother." She took off her work apron, exposing her pierced bellybutton. "You want to try that again?"

"Her brother, David, was there." I traced a path through

a pile of gravel on her worktable with my index finger. "He asked me to stay for dinner."

She deposited her dust into a container already filled to the brim with sawdust. "You have a crush on him, don't you?"

I thought about lying again, but decided against it. "Yeah, I like him."

"Okay," Helen said. "Let's go eat."

I frowned and followed Helen into the house. As she scrubbed the dust and grime from her hands, I could feel the knots forming in my stomach. Still silent, she made her way to the kitchen. I trudged behind her, slumped into a chair at the table, and waited for her to speak. She just rummaged through the refrigerator without even looking in my direction.

"Well, are you gonna give me a speech or not?" I finally asked.

Helen glanced at a label on the back of a jar of Alfredo sauce. "And just what speech are you expecting to hear?"

"You know, the *'You Should Be Careful'* speech. Or the *'You Shouldn't Mess Around With A Guy Like That'* speech."

"Why should I give you a lecture like that?"

I rose from the table and stood in front of my aunt. I wanted to look into her face, but I found myself staring at her linoleum floor. "You know why."

She lifted my face up with her hands and peered at me with soft green eyes. "Because the last rich boy you had a crush on ended up getting you pregnant?"

"Yeah," I whispered. "Because of that."

I hated that word: *pregnant*. Most of the time, I couldn't even bring myself to say it. Certainly, a girl that could say *Euclidian plane*, *dodecahedron*, and *deltoidal trihexagonal tiling* (my personal favorite) shouldn't have any problems uttering a simple word like *pregnant*.

"I can't tell you anything you don't already know." She pulled her hair into a ponytail and turned on the stove. "Just don't lie to me about it, okay? It's hard for me to be on your side when I feel like you're sneaking behind my back."

While she started preparing the sauce, I grabbed an onion from the fridge. Probably the only perk of not having a boyfriend was that I could eat as many onions as I wanted. Before cutting into it, I peeled off the old, brown layers. "I'm just tutoring Sarah long enough so she can get her grades back up. A few weeks from now, neither she nor her brother will remember I exist."

"Stop exaggerating." She glanced at me out of the corner of her eye. "So tell me about this David boy."

I knew my face was getting flushed—I could feel the heat radiating from my ears. There were so many things to say about David. He was smart, athletic, cute, charismatic...

I shrugged. "He's okay."

"That's it?"

"I've only spoken to him a few times. What else do you expect me to say?"

"So why didn't you stay?"

"Because I had plans with you."

She took the bits of chopped onion and dropped them into the Alfredo sauce. "You know, it's okay for you to start going out again."

"I'm too busy. I need to focus on my studies."

Helen sprinkled a few dashes of thyme to the mixture. "Isn't your prom coming up?"

"In a few months."

"Are you going?"

"Of course not."

Helen sighed. "Hand me the pasta out of the pantry, will you?"

I grabbed the box of fettuccine, and made a mental note of the location of a bag of cheese puffs. If we didn't start talking about something other than my social life pretty soon, those cheese puffs were living on borrowed time.

"Has Sarah made any decisions yet about the baby?" she asked as I handed her the pasta.

Okay, maybe I was better off talking about David.

"No, not yet."

"And how far along is she?"

"Almost eight weeks."

Helen looked out of the window. Although there was nothing but an old wooden fence with peeling white paint in front of her, it seemed like she was staring at something else. But what she was looking at, I didn't know. Maybe she was looking at the life that could have been. *My* life that could have been.

"You know you have to help her make a decision," she said.

I narrowed my eyes. "I won't force her to do anything she doesn't want to do." I could hear my voice getting louder as I spoke. "She has the right to make her own decisions."

"I'm not suggesting that you force her to do anything," Helen replied. "But she's got to make a choice, one way or the other. If she decides to have the baby, whether she gives it up for adoption or not, that's fine. But if she doesn't..." Helen let her words disappear into the steam rising from one of her pots. "It's better if she decides now rather than later."

I was nine weeks along when I finally told someone about my pregnancy. Up until then, I had been too scared to admit it. But as I broke down and told Helen the news, she said all the right words and did all the right things to comfort me. And more importantly, she sat beside me and held my hand when I broke the news to Dad.

It was three weeks later when Dad finally "encouraged" me to end my pregnancy. As caring and gentle as the doctor was, I still got sick to my stomach if I thought about the procedure too much.

After what seemed like an eternity, Helen turned back toward me with a goofy grin on her face. "I saved some magazines for you. I had to hide all the dirty ones, though." She winked. "I'll finish up dinner and call you when it's ready."

"Sounds good," I said, thankful to finally end our conversation.

I headed to the guest bedroom. After tiptoeing across a floor filled with cat toys and scratching posts, I slid into the closet. A stack of magazines sat on an old wooden trunk. I threw the magazines to the floor and pried open the lid. All of my paintings, sculptures, and art notebooks were as I had left them.

When most people at school looked at me, they probably thought I was just a chubby girl that liked to solve differential equations. But thanks to my mother, I also had an artistic side. The story was, one day Mom came home to find I had cut all the pictures out of her art books and pasted them on the wall. Dad was supposed to be watching me, but he was too busy staring at the back of his eyelids. Mom didn't punish me, though. She took photographs of my "masterpiece" and hung them on the refrigerator.

Over the years, I had dabbled in watercolors, pottery, and even photography. But after Mom died, I started making collages again. In a weird way, I thought it gave me a connection to her. Helen was great about it, always finding old books and magazines for me to cut up. She even let me keep my stuff over at her house. The last thing I wanted was for Dad to see some of my artwork.

I pulled my scrapbook of collages from the trunk and sat on the bed. I flipped through the scrapbook slowly, taking time to run my fingers over my work. Some of the artwork was almost seven years old, but I could still smell the glue on some of the pages. I got to the middle of the scrapbook and paused. There was a blank page. Well, almost blank. A big, fat, red "A" was plastered to the center of the page.

Like I said before, I hated the p-word. But there were other words I hated even more.

chapter[6]
the uniqueness(theorem)

I zipped down the hallway, a hall pass from my homeroom teacher in one hand and a thin, brown envelope in the other. I had never been in such a hurry to get to our school library. Of course, maybe if I had spent more time there, my SAT Verbal scores wouldn't be so abysmal.

As I turned down another corridor, I noticed Sarah, surrounded by what looked like the entire wrestling team, heading my way. I looked at her out of the corner of my eye, and even smiled a little when she got within speaking range.

Sarah didn't even look in my direction as she passed

by. I must have blended in with all the other short, black, female math tutors that occupied the hallway.

Not that I expected anything different. My life at school seemed to resemble something like this:

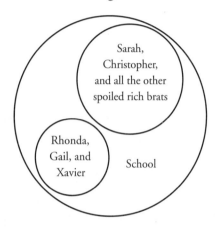

I brushed off Sarah's cold-shoulder routine and entered the library. Gail sat behind the checkout desk, her face hidden by a huge novel.

She peered over the top of her book as I neared her. "What are you doing here?"

Instead of answering immediately, I dropped my bookbag and pulled a letter out of the envelope. I slid my glasses farther up my nose and cleared my throat.

"Dear Ms. Lee," I began, sounding like I was a spokesperson in a toothpaste commercial. "On behalf of the Georgia Institute of Technology, we are pleased to inform you of your selection as a finalist in the President's Achievement Program, one of our—"

"Oh my God! Let me see!" Gail snatched the letter from me and pressed it to her face.

"Do you girls mind keeping it down?" Mrs. Brooks, the librarian, poked her head out of her office. "Don't forget where y'all are."

"Sorry," Gail whispered back, her eyes still on the letter, oblivious to the fact that Mrs. Brooks had already returned to her office. "Rhonda just found out she got a full scholarship to Georgia Tech."

"I haven't been awarded anything yet."

"It may as well be official," she said. "Now shut up so I can read this letter."

As Gail continued to read, I glanced around the room. I started to head toward the New Arrivals section, but stopped once I noticed Christopher McCullough and Tina Robbins, a freshman, browsing through the books. Christopher leaned over and whispered something to Tina, and just as I expected, she smiled, giggled back at him, and playfully slapped his arm.

I shook my head. Ever since Christopher and I broke up, I had made it my mission to avoid him as much as possible. I could almost sense him—it was like I had some type of radar. Whenever he was near, my skin began to crawl and my stomach began to boil.

"Rhonda, are you okay?" Gail asked, nudging my arm.

I snapped back to attention. "Yeah. Why do you ask?"

"Because your fist is balled up so tightly, your knuckles

are turning white. If that envelope was alive, you would have choked it to death."

I looked down at my hands and relaxed my grip.

"I guess you noticed Christopher," she continued.

I nodded.

"Forget about him—you've got better things to think about." Gail handed the letter to me. "I'm so excited for you. Why didn't you call me this weekend and tell me the good news?"

"I didn't open the letter until late last night. I spent Saturday night and most of Sunday at Helen's house, and before that I was tutoring—"

"When did you start tutoring on the weekends?"

"Just last week." I focused my gaze on the stack of books piled behind her. "He's just a middle school student. No one you know."

Why in the world did I just lie? Was it because I was protecting the fact that Sarah was getting tutored? Or was it because I didn't want to hear a lecture on how I shouldn't be fraternizing with the enemy?

Compared to public high schools, our class was pretty small. There couldn't have been more than one hundred and fifty of us—we all knew each other by name. But there was still an invisible line that divided those that came from normal backgrounds, and those that came from the "upper echelons" of society. Gail had had her own issues with the in-crowd at her old school, and she now avoided them as much, if not more, than I did.

Gail pointed at me. "I don't care when you opened that letter, you should have called me. We're supposed to be best friends. We're supposed to tell each other everything..." Her voice trailed off as she frowned and peered around me. "Listen, I'd love to discuss this further, but we're about to have an unwelcome visitor."

I turned around to see Christopher heading our way. His gaze locked with mine, and he hesitated.

For a second, I remembered how it used to be, when he'd stay up all night listening to me drone on about something. Or when he'd cut class just to see me during lunch. Or when after we'd sleep together, he'd hold my hand and let me snuggle beside him.

Then he winked at me, and I suddenly remembered that he was an ass.

As he started toward us, I grabbed my bookbag and threw it over my shoulder. "I'm not in the mood for a rendezvous with the ex," I said, already heading for the exit. "I'm out of here."

"Rhonda, don't run off." Gail rose from her seat. "You can't avoid him forever."

If I wasn't so busy walking toward the door, I would have stopped to correct Gail. I didn't have to avoid Christopher forever—only for six more months.

∴

I walked into the community center and was immediately swarmed with a barrage of hugs.

"Hey, Rhonda," the twins yelled.

Every Monday, I tutored my favorite students, twins named Keisha and Tasha. They were like a two-headed monster sometimes, the way they eerily spoke in unison and finished each other's sentences. With their hair full of little black plaits, glass beads, and multicolored ribbons, they brought color and energy to the drab, gray building.

I glanced toward the corner where their mother sat quietly, reading a paperback. She looked over the top of her book, flashed me a smile, and went back to reading. The chairs at the center were uncomfortable, but Mrs. James looked as if she could have been at a spa, she seemed so relaxed.

After I settled the girls down, we began to go over their math problems. It was a tedious process, going through each problem repeatedly. The two hours I spent with those girls was more tiring than running a marathon—backward. With their constant questions and non-stop fidgeting, it was a battle just to get through one problem, much less ten.

I loved every minute of it.

It was nearing the end of the tutoring day, and Sarah still hadn't shown up. She had left me a phone message saying she would be by to drop off something I left at her house last weekend. I didn't think I forgot anything, but I was in such a rush to leave, there was no way of really knowing.

As I glanced at my watch for the one-hundredth time, I heard a raspy voice behind me. "Sorry I'm late."

I looked up to see David Gamble standing over me. For a second, both the girls and I were quiet. It was probably the first time the girls had been completely still and silent since they were conceived. But a second later, their usual chatter burst through.

"Who are you?"

"Are you here to get tutored? You have to wait, 'cause Monday's our day."

"Are you Rhonda the Rhombus' boyfriend?"

I didn't know who blushed more, him or me. I cleared my throat. "Girls, this is David. I'm tutoring his sister. I'm not his girlfriend."

"Then can he be my boyfriend?" Keisha asked.

"No fair, I saw him first," Tasha replied.

I wanted to point out that *I* saw him first, but the last thing I needed to do was get into an argument with a pair of feisty twins.

"Why don't y'all share," I said, smiling.

The girls frowned for a second, before sticking out their tongues and making gagging sounds.

David squatted in front of the girls. "And what are y'all's names?"

"I'm Keisha—"

"And I'm Tasha—"

"And she's Rhonda the Rhombus."

David frowned and looked up at me. "What?"

I shrugged. "They're learning geometry." It wasn't much of an explanation, but it was the best thing I could come up with. I wasn't exactly happy with the girls associating me with such an unusual shape, but if it helped them with their homework, I'd get over it.

As if on cue, the girls began chanting my name in a singsong fashion. It was very cute, although it was safe to say the girls were no better at music than they were at math.

"Okay, I think it's time to go," Mrs. James said, in the midst of the third verse. Thankfully, most of the other students at the center had grown accustomed to the twins' constant singing and unruliness, so it wasn't that big of a deal.

"Bye, Rhonda," they said, their faces in a pout. They linked arms with each other and walked over to the corner, where their coats were piled.

David sat beside me. "They're full of energy."

"This is a good day. Most of the time, they're bouncing off the walls," I said. "Because of their ADHD, it's difficult for them to pay attention in class long enough to grasp concepts. They need a lot of extra help with their homework."

"How long have you been tutoring them?"

"Long enough." I paused to wave to the girls as they exited the building. "You're pretty smart," I continued, turning back toward David. "You ever thought about tutoring?"

David shook his head. "I wouldn't be a good tutor. Didn't Sarah tell you about how my previous tutoring experience went with her?"

"Just because you don't know how to tutor doesn't mean you can't learn," I said. "All you need is practice."

He winked at me. "And are you going to give me lessons?"

"Maybe." I felt my lips curl into a smile. "I bet I could teach you a lot of things."

Oh my God, was I flirting with him? I didn't even think I remembered how to flirt.

"I bet you could," he said.

There were a few seconds of silence between us that seemed more like hours. I dropped my gaze to the table and began stuffing my bookbag.

"Anyway, I came to bring you this." He reached into his pocket and pulled out a check. He slid it across the table and under my fingers.

I took one look at the check and wanted to plant a kiss on his cheek similar to the one he put on Sarah a few days ago. "This is for fifty dollars."

"If it's not enough…"

"Not enough? I was tutoring your sister in trigonometry, not teaching her how to disarm nuclear weapons."

"According to her, you're worth every penny." He smiled. (God, he looked so much better when he smiled rather than frowned. It should be against the law for guys as cute as him to frown.)

"Plus, if Sarah has to be tutored, I'd rather she be taught by someone pretty as opposed to the sixty-year-old man with the bad breath and potbelly that Mom was threatening to hire."

Did he just call me pretty? I began to smile, until I realized he was saying the same types of things Christopher used to say.

"I'd better go," I said. I stood up so fast I knocked my chair over. I cringed as it crashed against the floor. Why couldn't I slide out of a chair with elegance and grace, like skinny chicks?

Oh, I know, because I'm clumsy, awkward, and overweight.

David jumped to his feet and scooped up my chair. I hadn't realized how fast he was until now. He must have been a great athlete.

Christopher was a pretty good athlete as well.

"So when are you coming back over to the house?" David asked as he followed me out of the community center.

"Tomorrow afternoon."

"Good. Maybe you'll finally meet Mom."

From the few snide comments Sarah said about her mother, I wasn't exactly looking forward to meeting her. She made the devil sound like a saint.

"Sarah and your mother don't get along very well, do they?"

"Well…"

"Oh, I'm sorry." I brought my hand to my mouth. "I don't mean to pry. It's none of my business. Forget I asked."

"No, it's not a problem," he said, his teeth chattering.

He quickly blew on his hands. "Mom and Sarah don't see eye to eye on most things. Mom has her issues, just like the rest of us. But her bark is worse than her bite."

All too soon, we were at my car. I opened the door and dumped my bag onto the backseat.

"Thanks for walking me to my car."

"Thanks for tutoring my sister. You're very good."

I laughed. "You don't have to thank me. I get paid to be a good tutor."

He shrugged. "Everyone deserves recognition once in a while."

"I wish my dad felt the same way," I said.

David blew on his hands again. All the while, he kept his gaze on me. "Fathers have a tough time seeing all the good in their children," he finally said. "They can be real assholes sometimes."

"The way you talk, I'd think you dislike your father as much as Sarah dislikes her mother."

David's face contorted into a grimace. "Maybe I do."

"Why?"

David looked at me, with eyes as dark as blood. "You'd better go. I don't want you to catch a cold."

David's answer to my question wasn't the conversation ender I was looking for, but I figured it would have to do. Between the cold air and David's icy demeanor, I would end up a human pint of ice cream if I talked to him any longer.

Then David flashed me a smile that could have made

December feel like June. "Goodnight, Rhonda the Rhombus."

I rolled my eyes. "Now I guess you're gonna go around calling me that for the rest of the year."

"What's wrong with being a rhombus?"

I couldn't believe I was actually debating the merits of a geometric shape with David Gamble. "Most people don't even know how to spell *rhombus*, much less how one looks."

"I think the title fits you well. It implies that you're unique."

"You mean weird."

David laughed. "Hey, you're the math whiz. What's another name for a rhombus?"

"A parallelogram."

He shook his head.

"A rectangle? A square?"

David continued shaking his head as he walked toward his car.

I pouted and placed my hands on my hips. "A lozenge?" I yelled. "A kite?"

He opened his car door. "You're thinking too hard. But don't worry, it'll come to you."

I watched David peel away, before jumping in my car and doing likewise. I turned off the radio and recited every mathematical term I had ever heard. I almost ran two red lights, I was so caught up in thought. Later that night as

I plowed through my homework, doing my best to push David's puzzle out of my mind, Xavier called.

"I need some advice," Xavier said. "I think I'm ready to ask Michelle Jacobs out on a date."

Xavier had had a lot of crushes on a lot of different girls, but no one compared to Michelle Jacobs, his next-door neighbor. Xavier had been pining after her ever since he could walk. And to be honest, I wasn't really sure why. The only thing Xavier and Michelle had in common was their zip codes.

"Why are you now all of a sudden ready to ask her out?" I asked.

"Because she just broke up with her latest boyfriend. He was a drummer, of course."

Michelle attended a performing arts high school. She couldn't sing or dance, but she could play the hell out of a xylophone.

"According to you, Michelle is always breaking up with her boyfriend," I said. "What makes this time any different?"

"Because this time, he was the one that broke up with her. It's usually the other way around."

"So you want to be the rebound guy."

He was quiet for a second. Finally, he sighed. "I'd rather be the rebound boyfriend than not a boyfriend at all."

I thought about David and wondered would a guy still be considered the rebound boyfriend if there had been a three-year gap between relationships.

"And have you talked to Gail about this?" I asked.

"Of course not," he said. "I think Gail wants us to date the most boring, bland people on the face of the earth."

"She just doesn't want us to get hurt."

"I'm seventeen years old and I've never even been on a real date," he said. "I think I'll take my chances."

I laughed. "Well, I haven't been on a date in a while, so I'm not sure how much my advice is worth, but if you really want to date her, just ask her out. All she can do is say no."

"You know what, you're exactly right. I'm gonna ask her out tomorrow." He paused. "Well, maybe next week. Or now that I think about it, maybe I'd better wait for a few weeks, just to make sure she doesn't hook back up with the drummer."

I shook my head. I knew it would take Xavier at least another month to build up the nerve to ask her out. "Hey, before we get off the phone, let me ask you a question. Do you know another word for a rhombus?"

I began to repeat all of the terms I had already ruled out, but Xavier interrupted me halfway through my list. "Sorry, but I don't even know what a rhombus is."

I finished my conversation with Xavier and got back to studying. But after spending three hours poring through my textbook and not retaining any information (and still not thinking of another term for a rhombus), I conceded defeat and headed to bed.

And then, at 3:14 AM, it finally hit me.

A rhombus was also called a diamond.

chapter[7]
false(roots)

"So when am I going to meet Justice Gamble?" I asked as I peered over Sarah's shoulder. "I've been tutoring you for over two weeks, and I've yet to see her."

"You wouldn't be in such a rush if you knew the woman." Sarah's gaze alternated between her textbook and a calculator. "You're better off not knowing her."

David frowned at his sister, but didn't say anything.

I sat beside Sarah and glanced at the essay I was working on for the Georgia Tech scholarship. "It's just that this application is due in two weeks…"

"Don't worry," David said. "She'll write the recommendation for you. I won't let her forget."

"*We* won't let her forget." She slid her homework toward me. "Take a look. What do you think?"

Sarah's big make-up exam was tomorrow. If she passed, she'd be back in the C-range, and I'd be one step closer to attending Georgia Tech.

I was beaming by the time I finished checking her homework. "You're gonna ace your make-up exam tomorrow. You only missed one problem."

Sarah yanked her paper away from me. "I missed one?"

"Missing one out of twenty isn't that bad," I said. "That's still ninety-five percent you got correct."

Sarah grabbed her calculator and began reworking the problem. "I was sure I got this one right…"

David looked up from his pile of homework and winked at me. "Congratulations. You've turned my sister into a math junkie."

I was finally at the point where I didn't try to hide my extra folds of flab when I was around David. Unlike Sarah, he would at least speak to me when he saw me at school (which was much too infrequently, as far as I was concerned). Other than the trust fund, the big house, and the high-profile parents, he and Sarah were just like any other teenagers. Of course, if Gail were here, she would have reminded me that Christopher possessed all of these things as well.

Sarah was still punching numbers into her calculator when we heard someone unlock the front door. I glanced up from my essay. David and Sarah had stopped working on their homework long enough to share an intense, silent look.

David must have noticed the bewildered expression on my face. "It looks like you're gonna get your wish," he said. "Mom's home."

I could hear the loud, distinct tap of her heels as she made her way to the kitchen. Each footstep reminded me of a clock ticking down to oblivion. I glanced at Sarah out of the corner of my eye. Her face was glued to her midsection. She fidgeted with her clothes and sat up in her chair, no doubt to make her stomach look smaller. I looked down at my belly and considered doing the same thing.

Justice Gamble finally entered the kitchen. Her sandy-brown hair was long enough to be fashionable yet short enough to be manageable. She was supposed to be in her late forties, but the wrinkles made her look much older.

"Hey, Mom." David rose from his seat and pecked his mother on the cheek. "How was your trip?"

"It was wonderful," she said. "I love Washington at this time of the year." She quickly eyed Sarah and me before turning to her son. "David, be a dear and get my bags out of the sedan."

David nodded, took the keys from his mother, and left. As soon as he exited, the room began to feel chilly.

Justice Gamble stared at Sarah. Sarah looked at her textbook. Justice Gamble cleared her throat. Sarah turned the page.

"Hello, Sarah," her mother finally said, after removing her coat.

Sarah looked up from the table. "What are you doing home so early? I didn't think you'd show up until tomorrow." Sarah was firmly planted in her chair, and it didn't look like she had any intention of getting up and greeting her mother as David had.

"My meeting ended ahead of schedule," she replied to Sarah, although she wasn't looking at her daughter. She was looking at me.

Justice Gamble walked to the kitchen table, where I was frozen in place. "You must be the tutor."

"Her name is Rhonda," Sarah said.

"It's an honor to meet you, Justice Gamble," I forced from my lips while trying to flash Sarah a "cool off" look.

As she shook my hand, I swore I could feel my index finger snapping in half. "I'm supposed to be writing you a recommendation, aren't I?"

I nodded. "My scholarship application is due in two weeks. I'm actually working on one of the essays right now."

She released her death grip on my hand. "You're working on your application now? I thought you were supposed to be tutoring my daughter?"

Tiny drops of sweat popped up all over my forehead. "I'm only half-working on my application—"

"So you're half-working on your application, and half-tutoring my daughter," she said. "Keep that up, and you'll end up doing a half-assed job on both projects."

At this point, I just stared at the woman, my mouth wired shut. It was a lot easier not to stick a foot in my mouth if I didn't speak.

Then she broke into a roaring cackle. "I'm only kidding with you, Rhonda." She slapped me on the shoulder. "You'll find that all of us Yellow Jackets have a good sense of humor. And please, call me Ms. Gamble. I only like to be called 'Justice' when I'm in chambers."

I eked out a laugh. "Right. Of course."

Ms. Gamble proceeded toward Sarah. "And just how is my daughter doing?"

"Sarah's doing very well. She should have her average pulled up to passing after this next test."

Ms. Gamble shook her head. "I know she's smart. She's just not focused. She doesn't have the drive to succeed."

"You know, I *am* in the room," Sarah said. "You could talk to me like I was in here."

Ms. Gamble seemed immune to Sarah's complaints. "You could learn a lot from Rhonda," she said. "She's a straight-A student and is projected to graduate in the top two percent of her class. She's already amassed enough credit hours through her Advanced Placement courses that she could enter college as a sophomore. And she still finds time to tutor those less fortunate than her."

My mouth dropped open as Ms. Gamble named a few honors I had been awarded. My own father didn't know as much about me as it seemed she did.

She turned to me. "Don't be offended, but I couldn't

just hire you without doing some checking up on you." Ms. Gamble smiled smugly at me. "I must say, I was very impressed with what I learned about you. You remind me a lot of myself."

I smiled. "Thank you for the compliment."

"I hear that you plan to major in engineering," she continued. "You know, I got my undergraduate degree in mechanical engineering. I figured an engineering degree and a law degree would be an unbeatable combination."

I nodded quickly. "I read that you graduated number two in your class at Harvard."

It was Ms. Gamble's turn to look surprised. "I see that you've been doing your homework as well." She sighed and glanced at her watch. "Well, it's been a long day, so I think I will retire for the evening." She shook my hand again. "Rhonda, it was a pleasure meeting you. I look forward to writing your recommendation."

I grinned as she pumped my arm. As she released my hand, she looked down at her daughter. Sarah was still frozen in her chair, her gaze glued to the top of the table.

She zoomed in on Sarah's face. "Are you gaining weight? Your cheeks are getting fat."

Sarah sunk lower into her chair and draped her arms across her stomach.

Ms. Gamble shrugged and headed toward the hallway. "Just don't come complaining to me when you can't fit into your cheerleading outfit. If you're not responsible enough to keep your weight down, you can pay to get your own outfit altered."

Ms. Gamble disappeared out of the room, the tap of her heels finally muffled by the thick hallway carpeting.

"If she bothered to talk to me, she'd know how much I fucking hate cheerleading," Sarah mumbled, still looking down at the table. She sniffled and ran the back of her hand across her nose. "She's going to find out, isn't she?"

I paused from gathering my application papers. "You're nine weeks pregnant," I whispered. "Someone is eventually going to notice."

"I know it sounds crazy, but I figured if I ignored it, it would just go away." She laughed. "Isn't that the stupidest thing you've ever heard of?"

"Don't worry, I used to believe the same thing." I finished gathering my application and slipped it into a folder. "Are you gonna be okay?"

"I'll be fine. I just have a lot of thinking to do." She swiped a cookie from the table and stuffed it into her mouth as she rose from her seat. "Mom has been the same size for my entire life," she muttered. "God, I hate her."

We headed toward the front door. "Try not to take it too hard. I'm sure she means well."

Sarah frowned. "How can you say some bullshit like that?"

I had to take a step back, I was so surprised by Sarah's outburst. The scowl on her face eerily reminded me of the look her mother had had on her face moments before.

"I can't believe you're siding with her," Sarah continued. "Didn't you hear the way she spoke to me?"

"Ms. Gamble just wants what's best for you," I said. "She's a little callous, but she's still your mother."

"Why am I not surprised to hear you say that? My mother's known you for five minutes, and she's already named you her protégé."

"Sarah, that's not fair—"

"You're not supposed to take her side. You're *my* friend, remember."

Laughter sputtered out of me. "*Your* friend?" I rolled my eyes. "Let's be serious. I'm your tutor, not your friend. Other than when I'm tutoring you, we don't hang out together. You don't speak to me at school." I shook my head. "You've never even asked about my mom."

"What about her? She can't be as bad as my mother."

"Of course she isn't," I replied. "She's dead."

Sarah's mouth dropped open.

I opened the door. "I don't think you'll be needing my services anymore," I said over my shoulder as I headed toward my car. "And let your mother know I'll come by next week to pick up that recommendation."

I left Sarah, dumbfounded and pregnant, standing on her front doorstep. I didn't bother looking behind me as I started the car and sped off. There wasn't anything worth looking back at.

chapter[8]
inverse(equations)

My mother died when I was eleven years old. It was a normal Saturday morning, just like any other Saturday morning in Columbia. She was cooking breakfast when she realized she had run out of eggs. So, wearing a pair of faded sweatpants and with her hair stuffed into one of Dad's old baseball caps, she ran off to the store.

It wasn't until two hours or so later that Dad and I started to get worried. Mom usually got sidetracked when she went shopping—she never saw a sale she didn't like. But to be gone for so long was unusual. Just as Dad was walking out the door to hunt her down, the police showed up.

There had been a car accident. There were no survivors.

I remembered feeling very hateful. Sometimes I wished she had died from cancer or some disease like that. That way, we would have at least known she was going to die, so we could have said goodbye. Maybe that was mean, but it was the way I felt. Was it too much to ask for a daughter to be able to say a final goodbye to her mother?

As bad off as I was, Dad was infinitely worse. He fell into a deep depression. He didn't neglect the "important" stuff—he paid all the bills, went to all of the parent-teacher conferences, and even found time to punish me every now and then. But most of the time, he just floated through the day, struggling to get from one hour to the next. There were some days when he wouldn't say five words to me.

I ended up spending a lot of time with Helen during those first few months. If it weren't for her, I would still be trying to gather the courage to buy my first bra.

Dad finally got over his depression, and about a year ago, he started dating again. Of course, I hated all the women he brought home. Jackie, his latest girlfriend, was just as bad as the other women. And if I were lucky, she would exit our lives just like the rest of them.

Jackie and Dad had another date tonight. They had been seeing each other for six months, eight days, and fourteen hours (not that I was counting). Jackie was an elementary school teacher—her lone good feature.

Dad stood in front of the hallway mirror, picking microscopic pieces of lint from his coat. I was almost ten feet away from him, but I could still smell the aftershave radiating from his body.

I must have had a really nasty look on my face, because Dad just sighed and shook his head. "Jackie really isn't that bad, once you give her a chance."

"Where are y'all going?"

Dad turned away from me so I couldn't see his face. "Nowhere in particular," he mumbled.

In Dad-talk, that meant he and Jackie were going to have a quick dinner, followed by a night at her place.

"I'm going to finish getting ready," he said. "Let Jackie in when she arrives."

I nodded. Jackie hadn't even gotten here yet and I was already feeling horrible. I would have killed to be doing anything other than staying in the house. I hadn't spoken to Sarah for almost a week, but I would have rather been tutoring her than spending the night alone. And now that school was out for the next two weeks because of Christmas vacation, I felt more depressed than usual.

I had thought about calling Sarah a few times. But why couldn't she call me, I rationalized. She was the one that needed help. I was fine by myself.

During lunch, I had forced myself not to look in her direction. She probably wasn't giving me a second thought, so why should I worry about her? But worrying was the one thing I couldn't help but do. How did she do on her re-test? Did she remember the difference between the cosine and cotangent functions? Did she tell her mother about the baby?

I also thought about David. Did he miss me? I hated to admit it, but I missed him a lot. I had only really known him for a few weeks, but I was already addicted to that goofy smile and deep voice. Not that I didn't like hanging out with Gail and Xavier, but there was something about David that made my skin tingle, and I missed that feeling terribly.

The doorbell rang, bringing me out of the misery of my subconscious.

I opened the door. With her auburn highlights and stylish eyeglasses, Jackie looked much too hip to be dating my father.

"Hello, Rhonda." Her full, plum lips were a stark contrast to her light brown skin. "Is your father almost ready?"

"He'll be ready in a few minutes." I moved out of the way so she could enter the house.

Jackie sauntered through the kitchen and sat at the table. She wasn't a big woman, but she was very…sturdy. "What are you doing here on a Saturday night? Young, attractive girls like you should be out dating."

"I don't date."

"Why not?"

What was with Jackie? She wasn't supposed to be asking questions like that. (Plus, between her and Helen, they made it sound like I was the most pathetic person in the world for not dating.)

"I don't have time," I said. "I'm too busy with my studies."

"Is that so?" Her glasses slipped ever so slightly along the bridge of her nose. "Remember, there's more to school than books."

"Not for my daughter," Dad said as he walked into the room. "She's got to stay on top of her grades, especially if she wants to get into one of the top math and science schools."

Jackie stood up, and Dad walked over to her and pecked her lightly on the cheek. "You look nice," he said, barely above a whisper.

"Thank you." She brought her hand to her mouth and softly giggled.

After staring into Jackie's eyes for way too long (remind me to throw up later), Dad turned to me. "I left some money on my dresser if you want to order a pizza."

"I may hang out with Gail, if she calls me back." I would have called Xavier, but even he had a date tonight. He had finally summoned up the courage to ask Michelle Jacobs out, and surprisingly, she said yes.

Dad walked over to me. "If you do go out, be home by eleven," he said. Then Dad leaned over, and for a second, I thought he was going to kiss me on the cheek. Instead, he awkwardly twisted his body to the side and gave me a lame, lukewarm hug.

Of course, I wasn't surprised. Another part of my "punishment" was that Dad no longer showed me any real affection. His hugs were horrible, his kisses nonexistent. I didn't miss the cheek kisses, though. It was the ones he used to plant on my forehead, right before I'd catch the bus to school, or right after he tucked me into bed, that I really missed. Those were the ones he started giving me after Mom died.

After a few difficult moments, he straightened himself. "See you later."

"Goodnight, Rhonda," Jackie chimed in, before they left.

I listened as Jackie's car started up, and as they pulled out of the driveway. And then, there was silence.

∴

The "My Life Sucks" Equation

If:

$A \equiv$ one slice of pineapple and ham pizza

$B \equiv$ one glass of ice-cold ginger ale

$C \equiv$ one complete rotation of all 523 cable channels

Then:

$5A + 2B + 17C =$ Complete and Utter Boredom

I wanted to cut a back flip when Gail finally called.

"Finally, another human voice," I said after picking up the phone. "What are you doing? I've been calling you all night." Gail could have been picking fuzz from between her toes and still have had a more interesting evening than I was having.

"Sorry, I was out with Lewis. We plan on hanging out at my house for the rest of the night if you want to come over."

I groaned. The last time I hung out with Gail and Lewis, I wasted two hours watching a documentary about phytoplankton.

"I would have suggested that you call Xavier," Gail continued, "but I'm sure he's too busy making a fool of himself." She snorted. "Maybe Michelle felt sorry for him."

"Gail, that's not nice."

"The bad thing about all of this is that after she dumps him, we're going to be the ones that have to piece him back together," she said. "Come on, Rhonda. You know this isn't going to end nicely for Xavier."

"According to Xavier, Michelle is a really nice girl. And as you like to remind us, she's exactly the type of girl he should be dating. In other words, she's not part of the popular clique."

"But she's into artists," Gail said. "Xavier will be lucky if he lasts until spring break."

I sighed. "You know, you don't ever hear me or Xavier complaining about your boyfriend."

"Lewis is smart, safe, and dependable. What's there to complain about?"

"But you're not attracted to him."

"Of course I am. He's a genius."

"Okay, let me rephrase that. You're not *physically* attracted to him."

"For your information, I find him to be very handsome," she said. "Just today, I was complimenting him on his smile."

"You've been dating him for over a year, and you haven't done anything more than kiss him—if you've done that."

"Lewis and I are intellectuals. We don't need to clutter our relationship with petty, non-necessary physical contact."

"Gail…"

"He likes me for my brains, not my body," Gail said, her voice somewhat softer. "He isn't caught up with my looks."

"But you're pretty."

"That depends on whom you ask," she said, before clearing her throat. "Now enough talk about Lewis. Are you coming over or not?"

Gail and I talked for fifteen more minutes before finally deciding to go to the movies. After I hung up the phone, I went to my room and pulled an assortment of clothing from the closet. I grabbed my favorite pair of jeans. They were the ones that hugged my butt just the right way, so I looked more on the voluptuous side and less on the chubby side. As I changed clothes, I did my best to ignore my reflection in the dresser mirror. After slipping on my jeans, I finally succumbed to the temptation and looked at the mirror.

Not too bad. Maybe those extra sit-ups were paying off after all.

I looked at the turtleneck I planned to wear, before tossing it back on the bed and pulling a low-cut crimson blouse from the closet. Just because I wasn't into dating didn't mean I had to dress like it.

∴

So much for watching a movie. By the time Gail and Lewis picked me up, we were already running late. We got to the theater to find the movie was sold out. After being out of the house for a grand total of twenty-five minutes, I ended up right back at home, with a few slices of leftover pizza to greet me.

As I made a beeline to the refrigerator, I noticed the blinking light on the answering machine. I pressed the message button, expecting to hear Dad's voice, but instead, Sarah's voice slipped out of the machine.

"Rhonda, this is Sarah. Please call me when you get a chance."

I looked at the wall clock. She had only called a few minutes ago. I picked up the phone, and just as quickly I put it back down. Why should I call her? Sarah was nothing but a spoiled rich kid, and I was much better off not being her tutor. I was better off not knowing any of the Gambles. The mother was a tyrant, the daughter was a brat, and the son was a mistake waiting to happen.

That being said, I had been miserable all week. I didn't want to admit it at first, but maybe Sarah was right when she called me her friend. And as mad as I was, was I willing to destroy a growing friendship over a petty argument?

I picked up the phone and dialed the number. Sarah answered on the first ring.

"Hey, it's Rhonda."

There were a few seconds of silent agony on the phone.

"You called?" I asked.

"Um, yeah," Sarah said. "I just figured you'd want to know, I aced my test. I am officially passing trig."

I felt myself beaming and forced myself to frown. "Great." I made my voice as flat as a sheet of paper.

"That's it? I thought you'd be happy."

"What more do you want to hear? You passed. I'm happy."

Sarah huffed. "Fine. Be that way."

"Whatever."

Silence was the only thing flowing between us for a few seconds. Each breath seemed to hover on the receiver an extra second, as if it were deciding whether to become a word or stay a puff of air. I coughed a few times, but I couldn't bring myself to say anything.

"This is stupid," Sarah finally said. "Can you get out of the house tonight? Let's do something."

"Like what? Study?"

Sarah laughed so loudly, I had to move the phone away from my ear. "Rhonda Lee, it is eight o'clock on a Saturday night, and all you can do is think about studying?"

Technically, with Dad out all night, I could have walked in and out of that house as many times as I wanted. And I did say that I might be going out tonight. However, I was sure Sarah Gamble wasn't the type of girl he expected me to be hanging out with.

"I don't know," I said. "Dad is out for the evening, and I don't think he would approve—"

"You're saying you've never snuck out before?"

I winced. She had me on that one.

"Sorry," I said. "I just can't leave the house. I don't sneak out anymore."

Sarah paused for a second. "Well, then I'm coming to you."

My eyes widened. "What?"

"What's your address? I'll be over there in twenty minutes."

"Sarah, there is no way I'm letting you—"

"I'll bring David."

I opened my mouth to object, but my voice was caught in my throat.

"I miss hanging out with you," she said. "*We* miss hanging out with you. Can we come over? We won't stay long. Plus, we'll bring your recommendation letter."

I thought about how angry I was supposed to be at

Sarah. I thought about how cute David looked. I thought about how much I wanted that recommendation.

I thought about how lonely I felt.

So after all of that thinking, I said the only reasonable thing.

"Come on over."

chapter[9]
interpolation

Sarah said she and David would be at my house in twenty minutes. Twenty minutes wasn't a long time when you were sweating over a calculus problem. But when you were waiting for your friends to sneak over to your house, twenty minutes was an eternity. By the time they got here, I would have second-guessed myself enough times to give myself heartburn.

I got so nervous, I began gnawing on my toenails (I'm limber for a big girl). It was a habit I reserved for the most nerve-wracking times—waiting for my SAT results, hoping for a negative pregnancy test, etc. When the doorbell finally rang, I almost swallowed my big toenail.

I opened the door to see Sarah huddled on the porch. She smiled the most authentic smile I had ever seen and stepped inside the house.

"I'm so sorry," she blurted out, as her eyes began to tear up. "I didn't mean—"

"No, I'm the one that should be apologizing." I looked away from her, so I wouldn't start crying as well. "Wait—where's David?"

"That idiot was about to park in your driveway," she said. "Obviously, he's never snuck over to a girl's house before. I had him park farther down the street, along the road."

I made myself laugh, but in the back of my mind, I wondered if he was parking in the same spot Christopher used to park in.

Sarah stepped back and looked at me. "You look amazing."

I glanced down at myself. I hadn't realized I still had on my clothes from when I planned to go to the movies with Gail and Lewis. I felt myself blushing.

"Why don't you wear stuff like that more often?" Sarah asked. "You have a great body."

"My body's not great."

"Well, your breasts are great. I'd kill for a chest like that."

I brought my hands to my chest. As flattered as I was,

I didn't want Sarah Gamble giving commentary on my chest.

Just then, David came to the door. "Wow," he said.

Sarah yanked him inside and slammed the door shut. "If you're going to gawk, at least do it after you're inside the house."

David didn't respond. Maybe he was too busy staring at me.

"Doesn't she look good?" Sarah asked.

"She looks better than good." His eyes were on my face, as if he was trying to soak in every curve, every detail of my skin. The way David was looking at me, I *did* feel great. A look like that made all the sit-ups in the world worthwhile.

"This is for you." Sarah pushed an envelope into my hands. "Signed and sealed by the Judge herself."

I flipped the recommendation letter over and over in my hands, like it would magically disappear if I took my eyes off of it. I could already picture myself walking across the Georgia Tech campus.

"So now what?" Sarah asked, breaking me out of my trance. She pushed by me and sat on the couch. "Is anything on TV?"

"Just some mindless, run-of-the mill music videos," I said.

Sarah smiled. "My favorite."

I pulled myself away from David's gaze and sat down beside her. David hovered for a few seconds. There was just enough space on the couch for him to sit beside me, but we would have been pressed pretty close together. He instead sat across from us in the recliner.

Maybe I wasn't so "wow" after all.

"Where's your Dad?" Sarah asked, flipping through the same devoid channels I had perused earlier.

"Out on a date."

David looked at his watch. "When is he coming home?"

"Not until six or so in the morning."

Sarah laughed. "Oh, he's on one of *those* dates. Mom seems to have one of those every other weekend, doesn't she, David."

David didn't seem too pleased at Sarah's comment. "She's lonely."

"Aren't we all," she muttered, her face turned to the television.

"Is your mother out tonight?" I asked.

"No, she's at home," Sarah said. "She fell victim to too many martinis. When she stays in, that's what usually happens."

David's mouth was contorted into a long frown by now. "You shouldn't talk about her like that."

I sighed. I would be in enough trouble if Dad came home and found Sarah and David (especially David) here. He would be even madder if they had begun World War III in his living room.

I turned to David. "How is the basketball team doing?"

The deep furrows on his brow softened a little. "We're undefeated," he said. "Between me, Johnnie Chang, and Christopher, we've got a killer squad."

Just hearing that name slip from David's lips made me want to strangle him. I shoved my hands under my arms and balled them into fists.

"We should give Christopher and Johnnie a call," Sarah said, finally settling on one of the music channels. "Maybe we can swing by one of their houses once we leave here."

Just when I thought the furrows had disappeared from David's face, they returned, deeper than before. "There's no way I'm taking you to Christopher's house. He's not as nice as he appears."

"How do you know?" Sarah replied. "I know your teammates better than you think. Johnnie and I shared a class together, and Christopher—"

"Let's be clear about one thing: Christopher McCullough is the last person you need to be hanging out with," David boomed. "And I'm definitely not taking you over to Johnnie's house—not at this time of night. It's too dangerous."

Sarah rolled her eyes. "You're kidding, right?"

"East Columbia isn't safe." David shook his head. "Not that it matters. You wouldn't like Johnnie anyway. He isn't the type of person you'd hang around."

"Why? Because he's Asian?"

David responded with a dark, sarcastic, sinister laugh. "No, because he's poor. Aren't you the one who said if a guy didn't drive a Mercedes, he was beneath you?"

"Screw you, David." Sarah's eyes narrowed to two hazel buttons on her face. "That is *so* mean. It sounds like something Mom would say."

"It doesn't change the fact that it's true."

Sarah stood up so fast, I thought she was going to lose her balance. "Maybe I did say stuff like that, but that's in the past."

"You probably said that six months ago."

"A lot can happen in six months," she said.

"Enough!" I stood up and walked between them. "We're supposed to be having fun. If all y'all are going to do is argue, y'all can go back home."

David looked down at his feet. "Sorry."

"Yeah, me too," Sarah chimed in.

Even though they both apologized, I didn't believe either one of them. I headed toward the hallway. "Sarah and I are going to my room for a little while to talk," I said. "If you're hungry, there's some leftover pizza in the fridge."

David's mouth finally curved up a little. I smiled, and Sarah and I walked out of the room. I fully expected the pizza to be gone by the time we returned.

"Your bedroom is so cute," Sarah said as she followed me into the room. She immediately focused on the plush toys on my bed. "And your stuffed animals are adorable."

"They keep me company." I sat on the bed, tucking my legs underneath me. "What's going on with you and David? I've never seen y'all so mean toward each other."

Sarah sat on the bed and wrapped her arms around one

of my pillows. "Things have been pretty strained between me and David for the past week. He blames me for you quitting."

"Technically, he's right."

"Don't remind me," she said. "I must sound like such a spoiled bitch sometimes. Why didn't you tell me about your mother? I would have never been so insensitive if you had said something."

I shrugged. "It's private."

"But we're friends," she said. "At least, I thought we were."

"We are, sometimes." I took off my glasses and placed them on my nightstand. "When we're at your house, everything is great. But when we get to school, you act like you don't know me. It's like it's beneath you to come over and say hello."

"What? *You're* the one who doesn't talk to me." Sarah repositioned the pillow behind her back and placed her hands on her stomach. "You're one of the smart kids. Don't you know how much you guys intimidate us? The way you sit in your corner, eyeing everyone like they're too dumb to even breathe the same air as you." She shook her head. "I was always waiting for *you* to come over and speak to *me*. I thought you were ashamed to socialize with your students."

I'm not sure if she noticed it or not, but Sarah had begun rubbing her stomach in small, circular motions.

"The girls I sit with aren't my friends," she said. "At

least, not my real friends. If they were, I would have told them about this." She patted her stomach.

"Then why do you hang out with them?"

"Because my father is wealthy and my mother is a Supreme Court Justice. Their parents are wealthy and powerful people as well. It's just the way it's supposed to be, I guess."

As I looked at Sarah, my loneliness seemed to pale in comparison to hers. While Gail and Xavier were far from perfect, they were still my friends. I could count on them for almost anything.

Sarah grinned at me. "David was really excited about seeing you tonight."

I quickly stifled the smile forming on my lips. "Don't get me wrong—David's a nice guy. It's just that most guys are only interested in getting in your pants."

"That's not true," Sarah huffed.

"Oh, really." I pointed to her stomach. "And just how do you explain that?"

"That's different. I was in love."

"So was I," I replied. "That didn't stop Christopher from—"

I snapped my mouth shut, but it was too late.

Sarah frowned. "Is he the one that…"

"Yeah. He's the one." I thought back to our conversation earlier in the living room. "David's right about Christopher. You should leave him alone."

"He seems nice."

"He's an asshole."

Sarah shook her head. "If Christopher's really as bad as you and David say, why'd you even date him?"

I shrugged. "He made me feel important. He listened to me when no one else would." I tugged at the skin on my palm. "I know it's a stupid reason to date a guy, much less sleep with him, but—"

"It's not stupid," she said. "I probably fell for my guy for the same reason." Sarah glanced down at my bedspread. "And before you even think about it, please don't ask me who the father is. It's not something I want to talk about. I haven't even told him yet."

I nodded. While I was hoping she'd tell me who the father was, part of me really didn't want to know. Whoever's name she said, I would hate him for the rest of my life. Not that the guy did anything to me personally—I probably didn't even know him. But I would hate him nevertheless. It was just the way I was made, now.

Sarah cleared her throat and looked back up at me. "I've made my decision about the pregnancy."

I didn't have to ask what she had decided. I could already see the answer in her eyes.

"You'll need to pick a clinic," I said. "There are some good ones in-state, as well as in Georgia."

"Where did you go?"

"I went to a place in Atlanta."

"Were they nice?" she asked. "Were they gentle?"

I shrugged. "They made it as comfortable as they could."

"Then that's where I want to go," she said. "I've heard too many rumors about other clinics and about how much it hurt." She lowered her voice. "I don't want it to hurt."

"Sarah, you know I can't promise you that." I grabbed hold of one of my stuffed bears. "And since you're a minor, you're going to have to tell your parents."

Sarah chewed on her lip for a second. "My cousin just turned eighteen last month. She could be my twin, we look so much alike." She reached into her pocket and pulled out an ID card. "She gave it to me so I could buy cigarettes."

"Sarah, what we're talking about is a little more complex than buying cigarettes." I took the ID card from her. Sarah was right—she and her cousin looked exactly like each other.

"Will you go with me?" Sarah asked.

"Of course. I'd do anything for my friends." I handed the ID card back to her. "I'm gonna have trouble convincing my dad to let me go, though. Do you know anyone we can stay with in Atlanta?"

"Not anyone that I trust knowing my secret."

I sighed. "Gail may be able to help us, but I don't know if she will."

"Why not?"

I handed Sarah one of my teddy bears, as if that would cushion my words.

"Because she hates you."

chapter[10]
fuzzy(logic)

After two weeks of being bored out of my mind at home, school started back up. Gail had spent the majority of her vacation visiting family in Texas, so Monday was my first time seeing her since before Christmas.

We all met up at lunch, and things seemed normal enough. Gail sat on my right side, Xavier sat across from me. Xavier was passionately defending some abstract, outlandish theory. Gail was playing devil's advocate, just because she liked to argue more than Xavier did. I was happily eating a poor excuse for chicken parmesan (too much oregano, not enough basil). And then, everything changed.

"Hey guys."

I turned around. Sarah Gamble was actually speaking to me, in public. I quickly looked around the room. Weren't pigs supposed to be falling from the sky, or wasn't the earth supposed to crack open and swallow us whole?

"Hey, Sarah," I said. Even though we wore similar uniforms, there was no mistaking that Sarah wasn't supposed to be at our table. I grinned broadly as I looked back at Xavier and Gail. Their faces were anything but smiles, however.

"Um...hi?" Xavier's voice sounded as low and soft as a tuba could get (which wasn't very quiet at all, but it was quiet for him), and his face began to turn red.

"Hello," Gail said.

I waited for Gail to say more, but her lips were as frozen as the look in her eyes.

"So, are you coming over tonight?" Sarah asked.

I shook my head. "No, I've got to go to the community center tonight, but I'll come by tomorrow."

"Sounds good," Sarah said. "I'll tell David."

I looked at Xavier and Gail, hoping that they'd speak up. However, Xavier was too busy drooling on his tie and Gail wasn't even looking at Sarah.

"It was nice talking to y'all," Sarah said. She was working her southern belle, sweet-as-sugar voice for everything it was worth, but the only thing it was doing was turning Xavier into a beet. Gail showed no emotion at all.

Sarah finally left the table. The next few seconds were long, slow, and deadly quiet.

"Close your mouth," Gail said to Xavier. "You look like a damn fool."

Xavier snapped his mouth shut. His face was beginning to return to normal. "When did you start hanging out with Sarah Gamble?" he asked.

"A few weeks ago. I started tutoring her at the community center."

Xavier leaned closer to me, causing his sleeve to dip into his gravy. "Does she have a boyfriend?"

"You're pathetic," Gail said. "You sound like a horny teenager."

He shrugged. "I *am* a horny teenager."

"Sarah Gamble isn't your type," Gail said, before cutting her eyes at me. "She isn't *your* type either." She quickly stuffed her books into her bookbag and stood. Gail shook her head one final time, and left the table.

I guess I shouldn't have been surprised at Gail's reaction. Like me, she had been burned once before by the popular crowd. At her old school, she was teased mercilessly because of her Asian, Cuban, and African features. She had tried to ride it out, tried to laugh at the jokes, tried to pretend that the comments didn't bother her. But one day, after being teased yet again by one of the students in her math class, she snapped. Very calmly, she rose from her desk and proceeded to curse out every student in the room. When the teacher tried to intervene, she flipped him the finger and barged out of the building.

Gail's outburst cost her a three-day suspension. And when the principal forced her to apologize to her classmates upon returning to school, that just cemented into her head the notion that all popular cliques were evil.

While it wasn't exactly as intense as my incident, Gail's experience shaped her entire attitude toward high school life. Up until a few weeks ago, I had no reason to tell her she should feel differently. And even though I now had a great reason, I wasn't sure if that would be enough for Gail. It was barely enough for me.

∴

The center was at its usual capacity that afternoon—a handful of elementary and middle school kids were being tutored. I headed toward my table, but paused upon seeing Sarah, her face crammed into her textbook.

"What are you doing here?" I asked as I neared the table.

"Mom and I got into a fight." Although it looked like she had wiped away most of her mascara, there were still black smudges around her eyes. "I needed somewhere quiet to study."

"You know it's my day to tutor the twins," I said. "You may want to move to a different table if you're looking for peace and quiet."

"Compared to the way Mom shrieks, those girls won't be a problem." Sarah cleared away room on the table for me to put my books down. "Did you have a chance to talk to Gail?"

I shook my head.

"She really doesn't like me, does she?"

I sighed. "You knew what we were up against when we talked a couple of weeks ago."

"Do you still think she'll help me?"

"I don't know."

Just then, the James twins exploded through the door. I barely had a chance to stand before I was enclosed in one of their industrial-strength bear hugs.

"Hey, Rhonda," Mrs. James said, trailing behind her daughters. "Let me forewarn you, they're very hyper today. I made them take their medicine, but it doesn't seem to be doing any good."

"Don't worry, I'll be okay." I pushed the girls away from me and grinned at them. "And what are we studying today?"

"Fractions!" they sang.

Mrs. James retreated to her corner while I helped the girls pull out their books. Sarah stood to move out of our way. As she sat back down at the adjacent table, she placed her hands on her stomach, like she was nine months pregnant instead of three.

I wanted to say something to Sarah, but I was hit with a barrage of questions from the girls. Of course, none of the questions had anything to do with math, much less fractions. I eventually had to stop kidding around with them and give them my serious voice in order to get them to calm down.

I kept sneaking peeks at Sarah while I tutored the twins. I hoped we weren't disturbing her. Most of the other students had learned to steer clear of my table by now, on account of the loud, disruptive girls that always visited on Mondays. But Sarah didn't seem bothered by the noise. However, just because she didn't look upset didn't mean she wasn't distracted. Every time I glanced at her, it seemed like she was looking at us. She wasn't frowning or scowling, though. The way she stared at the girls, you would think they were her children.

We worked our way through the math problems, and by the end of the tutoring session, we had gotten a fair amount done. Unfortunately for Mrs. James, she would probably end up struggling for countless more hours just to help the girls finish the remainder of the assignment.

"I wish we could have gotten through more of the homework," I said to Mrs. James as the girls packed their bookbags.

"I'm just glad you got as far along as you did," she said. She had a smile on her face, but I could see how tired her eyes were. "At least I got a break for a couple of hours."

Sarah cautiously stood and walked next to Mrs. James. "Your girls are beautiful," she said.

Mrs. James nodded. "They're my little bundles of joy."

"I couldn't imagine trying to raise twin girls," Sarah said. Her voice was eager, but not pushy. "Especially with their condition."

"Honey, it's never easy. Even without their disorder, they'd still be a handful," Mrs. James said. "But don't be mistaken—I love those girls more than life itself. They're my babies, and their problems are my problems."

Mrs. James finished helping the girls pack their belongings. As they headed toward the exit, Sarah turned to me. "Rhonda, do you ever think about what you did? Do you ever wonder if you made a mistake?"

I began punching random numbers into my calculator. "I've never thought twice about it."

Even though I wasn't looking at Sarah, I could hear her drumming her pencil on the table. "I'm not having second thoughts," she mumbled in between taps. "I was just curious."

I nodded. Whether or not Sarah wanted to admit it, we could both hear the lie in her voice—and mine.

∴

I was bone-tired by the time I left the center. I was looking forward to spending a quiet night at home—just me, my calculus book, and a bowl of leftover stew. However, Gail seemed to have different plans.

She was waiting outside the house when I got home.

With her black leather coat and gloves, she looked like a loan shark coming to collect on an old debt.

I sighed and readjusted my bookbag on my shoulder as I walked to the door. I wasn't in the mood for Gail's theatrics. I knew the only reason she came over was to gripe about Sarah. And even if she had a legitimate complaint, I didn't feel like hearing it.

Gail met me at the front door. Her hair whipped across her face and fell over her eyes. She brushed it away to expose the same piercing stare that she had had at lunch.

"Do you have time to talk?" she asked.

I nodded. "How long have you been here?"

"Just a few minutes."

I unlocked the door and walked into the house. I picked up a handwritten note from the table. After reading it, I crumpled it and flung it into the trash. Dad had found some last-minute tickets to a basketball game at USC. He and the Teeny Bopper were going.

"Are you hungry?" I dropped my books on the table and went to the refrigerator.

"Is that all you have to say?" she asked.

"What do you want me to say?"

"How about explaining how you got to be friends with Sarah Gamble?" Gail yelled, like a long-burning firecracker that had finally exploded. "Since when did you socialize with girls like her?"

I emerged from the fridge with the bowl of beef stew. "Since a few weeks ago."

Gail's face had turned a reddish-orange hue. "She's a snob. She's a prissy, stuck-up bitch."

"You don't even know her."

"And you do?" She sunk into one of the kitchen chairs. "If y'all are such good friends, why is this the first time I'm hearing about her?"

"I was afraid you'd overreact."

"How the hell did you expect me to react?" Gail slammed her hand on the table. "You know how I feel about girls like Sarah."

"I'm sorry for the way they treated you back at your old school, but you've got to get over that." I sat across from her at the table. "Sarah's not like those other girls. She's a nice, sweet person, once you get to know her." I sighed. "And she needs your help."

"You expect me to help the girl that's trying to steal away my best friend?" Gail chuckled and rolled her eyes. "Good luck with that."

"Gail, she's pregnant."

Gail's mouth dropped open as she stared at me for a few seconds. Then, she shrugged.

"That's what she gets for being a slut."

If I were within arm's reach of Gail, I would have slapped her. I didn't know if I was mad or shocked or disappointed, but I did know that hitting her would have made me feel a lot better.

"So I guess that's the way you feel about me?"

Gail quickly brought her hand to her mouth. "Rhonda, I'm so sorry. I didn't mean—"

"Sarah *is* right. We're just as bad as those high-and-mighty cheerleaders, the way we talk about people. The only difference between us and them is that they're popular."

For the first time in ages, Gail and I were stuck in a room with nothing to say to each other. The Grand Canyon may as well have been between us, for as far apart as I felt from her right then.

"Maybe I should go," Gail said.

I didn't say anything as Gail headed toward the door. She paused after she reached the doorway.

"What type of help does she need?" she asked. The volume of her voice had finally returned to normal.

"She wants to end her pregnancy. There's a clinic in Atlanta that'll perform the procedure."

Gail leaned against the door. "Unless she thinks I'm a doctor, I don't see how I can help."

"She wants me to go along with her, and the only way I can think of going was if I go with you. Since your sister lives in Atlanta, I figured we could say she was giving us a tour of Georgia Tech that weekend."

Gail shook her head. "You want me to lie?"

"Yes."

"Why do you have to go? Doesn't she have any other friends?"

"No."

Gail crossed her arms. "And why should I help her?"

110

"Because I'm your friend, and because I'm asking you."

I could almost see Gail's mind churning away as she processed everything I had told her. With Gail being the analytical person she was, I knew she wouldn't come to any decision tonight.

Gail and I talked for a few more moments, about nothing in particular, before she left. And after a day that was more melodramatic than two soap operas, I finally had the house to myself.

The funny thing was that as I ate my food in silence, I realized the last thing I really wanted was to be alone that night.

Side-Side-Side Congruence

If the sides of one triangle have the same lengths as the sides of another triangle, then the triangles are said to be congruent. The triangles will have the same size and shape, despite any translation or rotation of the objects.

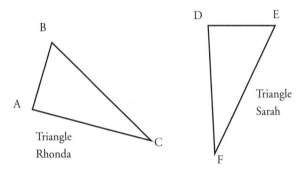

If:

Segment AB ≅ Segment DE ≡ number of ginger tablets needed to quell morning sickness

Segment BC ≅ Segment EF ≡ number of pounds gained in the first month of pregnancy

Segment CA ≅ Segment FD ≡ number of appointments made at the Women's Clinic of Atlanta

Then:

ΔRhonda and ΔSarah are congruent.

chapter[11]

congruence

Sarah was jumping up and down like a kid on Christmas morning as I helped her pack her clothes. "I've never had a real sleepover before," she said. "Mom didn't trust a lot of my friends around her expensive furniture."

"I don't know if I would quite consider this a sleepover," I said. "We have to leave early in the morning and it makes it easier if we're at the same place."

"Is Gail staying over at your Aunt Helen's house as well?"

I shook my head. "Gail isn't that comfortable around you yet."

"Will she ever be?"

I didn't have to think twice. "No."

Sarah sighed. "At least she agreed to help me. What made her decide to do it?"

"Gail will do anything for her friends."

"But I thought she didn't like me."

"She doesn't. She's doing it for me."

A sad smile came to Sarah's face. "She sounds like a good friend. You're lucky."

Once again, I could feel the loneliness that seemed to fill Sarah's life. I patted her on the shoulder. "Ready to get out of here?"

She nodded. "Too bad it's a girls-only party," she said, coyly. "I know you'd love it if David could tag along."

I frowned. As cute as I thought he was, I was *not* ready for him to see this out-of-shape body stuffed into a pair of pink pajamas.

Sarah opened her door. "David," she yelled, "I'm about to leave."

David bolted down the hallway. For the past half-hour, David had been claiming that he was about to go shoot some hoops, but he never came close to stepping foot outside. He dribbled his basketball against the carpeted floor a few times before palming the ball and stuffing it under his arm. "I wish you could be here to see us play this weekend," he said.

"You know I hate basketball," Sarah replied.

"I wasn't talking to you."

Suddenly, it felt like I was standing in the middle of the Sahara, sweating my life away. "Maybe next time," I said. I found myself staring at the basketball instead of looking at him.

"Since when did you become interested in Georgia Tech?" David asked.

We were all quiet for a few seconds.

He nudged Sarah. "Now I'm talking to you."

Sarah laughed and gave off a sheepish grin. "I don't know. I figure I have to start thinking about college at some point."

"I thought you were thinking about going to Francis Marion University, like me."

Sarah shook her head. "Just because we're related doesn't mean we have to go to the same college. We're allowed to have different lives."

David took a step back. "I know, but—"

"Anyway, if Rhonda ends up going to Georgia Tech, you will have transferred there before the middle of the semester."

He winked at me. "Georgia Tech *is* a pretty good school."

Again, I focused on the basketball as it sat sandwiched between David's lean, muscular torso and his sculpted arm.

Sarah leaned over and elbowed me in the ribs. "Now you're supposed to flirt back."

I picked up a pillow from her bed and whacked her across the head, but was sure not to really hurt her. "I'm flirting on the inside," I said, before sticking my tongue out at her.

David looked at his watch. "I'm late." He reached out and hugged Sarah. "Y'all be safe."

Sarah rolled her eyes, but still returned her brother's embrace. "We'll be sure to sleep with the lights on."

David hugged me as well. "Keep Sarah out of trouble."

I nodded. Either I was helping her get out of trouble, or I was getting her into more trouble than she had ever experienced.

David grabbed Sarah's suitcase, and we all shuffled out of her room.

We got to the kitchen door, and I tapped Sarah on the shoulder. "Aren't you going to say goodbye to your mother?"

"I haven't spoken to her in two days. I'm not about to start now."

I let David walk a few steps ahead of us. "You didn't tell her, did you?"

"There's nothing to tell," she said, before shrugging. "At least, there'll be nothing to tell after this weekend, right?"

∴

"Where's Sarah?" Helen asked as I entered her work shed. The sky was dark and overcast, but Helen's industrial floodlights basked her entire backyard in a sea of artificial moonlight.

"She's taking a shower. I figured I'd come out and check on you. What are you doing?"

"Sweeping."

I frowned. The only time Helen cleaned her work shed was when she had too much on her mind to be creative.

Helen pointed to a pile of clay pots in one of the corners of the shed. "You can help by separating the good ones from the bad."

I looked toward the corner. I'd be lucky to find one good pot out of the twenty or thirty stacked on top of each other.

"Thank you for not saying anything to Sarah about the pregnancy," I said.

"I did as you asked."

I had to beg Helen not to say anything to Sarah about our plans to sneak to Atlanta. Sarah had enough pressure on her without someone else throwing in his or her two cents. Not that what Helen would have said was bad—I just figured it was unnecessary at this point. Sarah had made her choice, and we had to respect that.

"You don't approve of our plan, do you?"

"Do you expect me to approve of you lying to your father and sneaking an underage girl across state lines to terminate her pregnancy?"

I gulped. "That's not quite how I would put it."

She brushed a few wisps of hair from her face. "I'm just glad you didn't try to convince me to go with you."

"I thought about it, but I didn't want you getting into trouble if things didn't turn out as planned."

"I'm not the one you should be worried about." Helen's usual jovial grin had been nonexistent the entire evening. Instead, her pink lips formed a hard and stern line across her face. "Sarah could get into a lot of trouble."

"She's already in a lot of trouble," I said. "And if I don't go with her, she'll go anyway. By herself."

Helen stopped sweeping and leaned against her broom. "Are you sure she's ready for this? It's not like she can change her mind halfway through the procedure."

I fought the temptation to roll my eyes. "Don't forget who you're talking to. I know what she's getting herself into."

"But does *she* know?"

"I don't know," I said. "But at least she's the one making the decision."

Helen propped her broom against the wall. "You'll need to make sure she gets on some type of birth control after she's recuperated."

"I plan to take her with me the next time I go to the clinic," I said. "With an allowance like hers, she shouldn't have any trouble affording birth control pills."

The work shed was only a few yards wide, so it only took Helen a few steps to traverse the room. "You know, those pills would be a lot cheaper if you covered them with your father's insurance."

"No. What I do with my body is none of his business."

She smiled at me, but not in a happy way. "You still blame your father, don't you?"

I wiped my mouth with the back of my hand. I could feel my tongue turning to paste. "He made me do it."

"He was only doing what he thought was best."

"It's my body."

"But you're his child."

I snorted. "No man has the right to tell a woman what to do with her body."

"But don't you see? You weren't a woman. You were only fifteen. Did you really think you were mature enough to have a child at that age?"

I shrugged. "I guess we'll never know."

Helen reached out and gave me a hug.

"You do realize you're covering me in dust," I said.

She patted me on my back, surrounding us in a dust storm. "That's why God created showers."

I left Helen in the shed and headed back to the house. Sarah was in the living room, petting one of the cats and flipping through the five television channels that Helen got with her standard TV antenna. She looked like she could be a twelve-year-old, the way she was curled up in her pajamas on the couch. She looked too innocent to be pregnant. But, I had probably looked the same way.

"You finished outside?" she asked once she noticed me.

I nodded. "Come with me. I want to show you something."

I led Sarah from the living room to the guest bed-room. I motioned for her to sit on the bed while I pulled my scrapbook out of the trunk in the closet.

"It's kinda like a diary with pictures," I said as I placed the scrapbook in her lap.

Sarah tried to hand it back to me. "If it's that personal, I don't want to look through it."

I shook my head. "I want you to look through it."

Sarah opened the book and pointed to a photo. "Is that your family?"

"Yeah." I began pointing out pictures. "That's Mom and Dad from college. There's Helen." I slid my finger to the corner of the page. "And there's me, without teeth and in need of a diaper change."

Sarah laughed and continued to flip the pages. As she looked through the book, I gave her a history lesson on each page. Finally she got to the page I was waiting for her to see.

She ran her fingers along the large, solitary "A" glued to the page, just as I did every time I looked at the scrap-book.

"I guess you don't need a college degree to figure out what the 'A' is for," I said.

Sarah closed the scrapbook. "Why did you do it?"

"I was too young to have a child. Dad and I thought it was for the best."

"That makes sense—"

"I'm sorry." I finally looked at her. "I'm lying."

Sarah didn't say anything. Her eyes told me to take all the time I needed.

"It wasn't my decision," I continued. "Dad made me do it. *He* thought I was too young to have a kid. *He* thought it would ruin my future."

"He was probably right," Sarah said.

"Maybe." I reached over and grabbed her hand. "Are you sure about this?"

"I think so."

"I just don't want you to have any regrets."

As Sarah smiled, her lips trembled a little. "It's too late for regrets, isn't it?" She handed the book back to me. "I'd better get to sleep. I have a big day tomorrow."

Sarah pulled back the blanket and crawled into bed. Just like my father used to do, I leaned over and gave her a peck on the forehead. I could only wonder, if I hadn't ended my pregnancy, would I be doing the same thing to my son or daughter every night?

chapter[12]
the vanishing(point)

At exactly six o'clock, Gail pulled into the driveway. Sarah and I were already up, with our luggage collected in the kitchen.

"Hey, Gail," I said as she entered the house. "I should have known you'd be on time."

She cut her eyes at Sarah. "Have I ever let you down?"

"Nice to see you again, Gail," Helen said. "Do you want anything to eat?"

Gail inhaled deeply, before looking at her watch. "Sure, I'll take a few bites."

"That's good," Helen said, nodding toward the table, "because I already fixed you a plate."

Gail eyed the steaming plate, which happened to be next to Sarah. Gail stuck her head up and marched to the table. She then very deliberately slid her plate to the other side of the table and sat down.

"Good morning," she said to Sarah.

"Morning," Sarah replied back. Sarah's trademark accent seemed to make Gail frown even more.

"Why aren't you eating?" Gail said.

Sarah looked down at the table. "The nurse told me I couldn't eat this morning."

That made Gail sit back. Maybe she had forgotten why we were going to Atlanta in the first place.

"What time is your appointment?" Gail asked, a little quieter.

"Eleven o'clock."

"Then we'd better get going." Gail rose from the table and stuck a piece of bacon in her mouth. "We still have to stop by my sister's place."

We trudged out of the house and into the foggy, cold morning air. Gail pulled her suitcase from her trunk and dumped it into mine. Sarah had positioned herself at the front passenger side door, but with one look from Gail, she quickly retreated to the back seat.

I jumped in and started the car. I was glad I had a

good collection of music, because something told me there wouldn't be a lot of conversation on the three-hour trip.

As I pulled out of the driveway, I looked at Helen through my rearview mirror. From the way she leaned against the handrail, to the rollers in her hair, to her fuzzy green housecoat, she looked exactly like she had looked when Dad and I had made our trip to Atlanta.

∴

The nice thing about the quiet drive was that I had time to think about what Sarah was doing, and the part I was playing in it. Was she mature enough to make this decision? Should her mother have been informed? I had tossed and turned most of the night, contemplating whether I should call her mother or not. I had awoke a few hours later with my hands still wrapped around the cordless phone.

Sarah spent most of the trip faking a nap in the backseat, while Gail reread the same ten pages of a novel. Apparently, I wasn't the only one nervous about what we were getting ourselves into.

Gail had assured us that her sister spent more time at her boyfriend's house than she did at her own apartment, so Sarah would have plenty of privacy. When we arrived at the apartment, Gail's sister stayed long enough to hug Gail and slip a key into her palm before she darted across town to see her boyfriend. We invited Gail to come along with us to the clinic, but being the genius that she was, she wisely declined.

Fifteen minutes after we left the apartment, we were there. The parking lot was surprisingly full. I didn't know whether we should be happy or sad about other people being in our situation.

I had prayed every night for the past three years that I would never see this place again. But here I was, walking across the same asphalt desert toward the building of my salvation. At least I wasn't the one having the procedure this time. Lucky for me, unlucky for Sarah.

"So this is it?" Sarah asked.

Although I didn't have to, I looked at the silver-plated numbers attached to the red brick face of the building. "Yep, this is the place."

"It's not quite what I was expecting."

I almost laughed. "What did you think it would look like?"

"I don't know. It doesn't even look like a hospital."

"It's *not* a hospital."

The one-story building could have housed a law firm just as easily as it could have housed a women's clinic. There were no protesters in front of the building, thank goodness. Sarah was having a hard enough time walking in, without a barrage of people yelling at her.

Forget Sarah—*I* was having a hard enough time just

being there. It was so…quiet. Although it was almost ten in the morning, it sounded like the entire city was asleep.

Sarah teetered at the edge of the sidewalk running in front of the building. "How long until my appointment?"

I looked at my watch. "Five minutes closer than when you asked me five minutes ago."

"I'm sorry."

"Sorry for what? Being nervous? I'd be more concerned if you weren't." I wrapped my arm around her shoulders. "Let's drive around for a while. Maybe we'll even find an ice cream shop around here."

"I can't eat before the procedure, remember."

I cringed. "Sorry, I forgot."

We walked away from the building in slow, timid steps. I couldn't speak for Sarah, but I wanted to run as fast and as far away from the clinic as I could.

We got back in the car, but I didn't start the engine. "Sarah, it's not too late to change your mind."

"I know."

I began turning the key in the ignition, but Sarah stopped me.

"Am I doing the right thing? What if I'm making a mistake? What if—"

"Sarah, this is your life. Whatever questions you have about this, I can't answer."

She nodded and let go of my hand. "Let's go for that drive."

"Will you be ready to go in when we get back?"

She shrugged. "I don't know. Will you wait with me?"

"Of course."

"For how long?"

"For as long as it takes."

"And what if we never go inside?" Sarah asked.

I finally started the car. "Then we go back home."

chapter[13]
approaching(normalcy)

Two weeks after our trip to Atlanta, things were pretty much the same as they had been before. I still helped Sarah with her trig homework. Gail and Sarah still didn't get along, but at least Gail and I were back on good terms. I was still infatuated with David. And most importantly, Sarah was still pregnant.

We must have sat outside that clinic for three hours. Sarah would come close to going inside, but she could never quite enter the building. She wasn't ready to make a choice like that. I was glad she was mature enough to realize it. I didn't know if I would have been as mature if I were in her situation.

Of course, in typical Sarah fashion, she still hadn't told her family about the pregnancy. She wanted to have one last weekend of freedom before she told David and her mother and "all hell broke loose."

Sarah's plan was to go to the basketball game that Friday night and then go to a house party afterward. I was looking forward to going to the game (and seeing David in those shorts), but going to the party was a different matter. It had been so long since I had gone to a house party, I was afraid my body was allergic to music. And even if I did find the courage to dance, who would dance with me? David wasn't the partying type, so there was no hope of wrapping my arms around him. Knowing my luck, I'd spend most of the night hiding in a corner.

However, all the anxiety I was having over the party was nothing compared to the worry I got from Dad right before I was about to leave for the basketball game.

I placed my hands on my hips. "What do you mean that you and Jackie are going to the game? When did you decide this?"

"Earlier today," he said as he stared into his bedroom mirror and combed his hair. "I've heard a lot of good things about the basketball team. I figured it would be a good game."

"Dad, you haven't been to a basketball game at my school since my freshman year."

His gaze locked with mine through the reflection in the mirror. "Neither have you."

I winced. "Well, why didn't you say anything earlier?"

"Like I said, we decided at the last minute." Dad put his comb down and turned around. "Do you still plan on going to that party tonight?"

I nodded.

"Who are you going with?"

"Sarah."

Dad searched my face, as if he was looking for a lie. "Gail isn't going?"

"No. She isn't into high school parties."

"She sounds like a smart girl." He turned back to the mirror. "I'm sorry, but you can't go—"

"—Dad!"

He sighed. "You can't go unless I meet Sarah first. Will she be at the game?"

I nodded.

"Good," he said. "Jackie will be here in a few minutes. You can ride with us to the school."

I trudged back to my room. I should have been happy that Dad was going to a game with me, right? I mean, I had been complaining for years that we didn't do enough together. I just wished it were me and him going—not me, him, and his *mistress*.

I called Sarah and told her I'd meet her at the game. She actually sounded happy to be finally meeting my father. Compared to her home life, Dad and I were the All-American Family.

I looked at myself in the mirror. My clothes were all new, thanks to a shopping trip with Sarah. The hunter green sweater I wore fit exactly the way it needed to. It hid the rolls at my stomach, and it made my chest look curvaceous.

Sarah had bought one just like it, to hide her growing mid-section.

∴

The gymnasium was at a full roar when Dad, Jackie, and I walked in. The teams were only warming up, but people were already cheering. We were the best-ranked team in the conference, and we were playing the second-best team. Both sides of the gym were full of students and parents. I looked around for Sarah. After a few seconds, I caught a glimpse of her. She was parked behind our team's bench, and it looked like she had managed to save a few seats.

I led Dad and Jackie over to her. "How did you end up getting these seats?"

She smiled. "I told everyone that my mother was coming, and she was bringing a congressman from Virginia. So if anyone asks, your dad is a Democrat from Fairfax."

I laughed. "Dad, this is my friend, Sarah Gamble."

Dad shook Sarah's hand. "It's nice to meet you," he said over the crowd. "I've heard a lot about you."

Sarah slyly glanced at me. I knew she was wondering if I had told Dad about her pregnancy.

"I told Dad how much better you're getting at trig," I said. "I haven't told him about your problems with *geometry*."

Sarah nodded. "Your daughter is a great person," she said to Dad. "She's one of my best friends."

As Jackie introduced herself, I searched the floor for David. I finally saw him, just as he was charging toward the basket. As handsome as he looked up close, he looked just as good running across the floor, with his light brown legs pumping like the pistons in a muscle car. Every time he released the ball, his stroke was flawless. Whoever coined the term "poetry in motion" must have seen him play basketball.

"What are you staring at?" Dad yelled in my ear.

I shifted my gaze away from the court. "Nothing in particular."

I wasn't sure if Dad believed me or not. He just nodded and went back to watching the warm-ups.

As much as I wanted to pretend that he didn't exist, I eventually caught sight of Christopher. He was just as attractive, if not more so, than David. Looking at Christopher, you couldn't fault anyone for falling for him the way I did.

After a few more minutes, the game started. It was a pretty close first half. Every time our guys scored, everyone in our section of the bleachers jumped up and screamed at the top of their lungs. Whenever David made a basket, I gave a little more pizzazz to my cheer. And when Christopher scored, I barely clapped and forced myself not to frown.

Throughout the game, I could feel Dad's gaze on me. He was almost watching me more than he was watching the game. What he was looking for, I wasn't sure. Maybe he could tell I was cheering a little bit too much for David. I did notice that when Christopher scored, Dad didn't cheer at all. Actually, every time Christopher touched the ball, Dad looked like he wanted to jump onto the court and strangle him.

Halftime came and Dad left to get some popcorn. I was tempted to follow him to make sure he wasn't sneaking off to the locker room to beat Christopher into a bloody pulp.

"I love your sweater," Jackie said.

I turned to Jackie. Was this her lame attempt to connect with me?

"Thanks."

Jackie continued on, ignoring the flatness in my voice. "To be honest, I'm not a big fan of basketball."

I frowned. What did Dad see in her? Any woman that didn't like sports was a woman that didn't need to be with my father.

"Then why do you go to games with him?"

"With your schedule, your father says he doesn't have anyone else to go with."

My schedule?

I shrugged. "I'll have to remember to pencil Dad in," I said, in the most sarcastic way possible.

Jackie didn't have very long to sit there looking uncomfortable before Dad reappeared. He sat down and wrapped his arms around her. It was sweltering in that gym, yet he still felt compelled to smother her. I didn't know whether to be angry or jealous.

Halftime ended and the game continued at the same frenzied pace as the first half. As I cheered, I started to remember how much I loved going to games. For me, watching basketball was just as exciting as actually playing myself. I got an adrenaline rush just by looking at the players scramble for loose balls.

Sometime during the course of the second half, Dad managed to dislodge Jackie from under his arm and talk to me.

"Our center has to do a better job defending the lane," he said.

"I know. We're giving up too many rebounds."

Dad jumped up as the center leapt for the ball. "Get on the boards!" he yelled to the court.

"Box out!" I screamed.

The center did as we instructed, and got the rebound. He shot an outlet pass to a streaking David Gamble. David easily banked the ball off the backboard and into our basket.

Dad smiled and gave me a high-five. Those few words

we shared happened to be the best conversation we had had in three years.

Our guys started pulling away in the final five minutes, so the game was very anticlimactic during the last few possessions. But we were going to win, which was the most important thing. And I had my father back, for at least a few minutes.

Then the buzzer sounded, the game ended, and Dad slipped back into his usual self.

"What time is this party over?" he asked.

I shrugged. "Around twelve."

"Who's throwing it?"

"One of the girls in my class," I said.

He peered down at me and folded his arms.

"Julie Potts," I said. "She's class president."

Julie and I weren't great friends, but we got along pretty well. She was the type of person that could invite anyone to her party and make them feel welcome.

I had told Dad all the particulars about the party beforehand. For a fairly intelligent man, it was amazing how quickly he forgot things. He was probably too busy thinking about Jackie instead of listening to me when I talked to him about the party earlier that week. The only reason he allowed me to go was because he knew Julie's parents.

Jackie leaned closer to Dad and wrapped her fingers through his. "She's eighteen," she whispered. "She'll be okay."

What was this? The Teeny Bopper was actually taking

up for me. Knowing her, she just wanted to have a quiet night with Dad all to herself, without me around.

Dad snorted as he looked back at me. "Be home by eleven."

"Samuel," Jackie cooed. "The party doesn't end until twelve. At least let Rhonda stay until the end of the party."

Dad chewed on his lip for a second, before nodding. "A quarter after twelve," he instructed. "Not a minute later."

Now, at this point, most normal daughters and fathers would have hugged and had a picture-perfect moment. Dad and I weren't quite there, however. He just patted my shoulder, and that was the extent of our father-daughter connection.

chapter[14]
constants never(change)

Seconds after Dad and Jackie left the gym, Sarah turned to me. "Wow. You said your Dad could be strict, but I didn't think he was going to grill you like that," she said. "Do you think he'll freak out once you tell him I'm pregnant?"

I nodded. "He'll probably think I'll get pregnant, too. Like it's a disease you can catch from close contact."

She laughed. "You can catch it from close contact, although it's a lot closer than you and I will ever be."

Sarah and I left the gym, grabbed a burger, and headed to Julie Potts' house. I felt like I was in seventh grade and was going to my first school dance. I was going to rub the skin off my hands if I wrung them together any more.

Sarah parked behind the long row of cars piled up along the side of the road. The Potts' closest neighbors were almost a quarter of a mile away, so there would be no complaints about noise. We wrapped ourselves in our coats and briskly walked to the front door.

"Hey, Julie," I said as she opened the door.

Julie had a smile as sweet as Sarah's. However, she had enough makeup on to pose as a mime. She wore a sleeveless, V-cut blouse that plunged a little too deeply.

"Come on in," Julie said, her short, brunette hair bouncing as she talked. "Soda and punch are in the kitchen if you're not drinking alcohol. The beer is in the tub of ice on the floor. If you're going to smoke, do it outside."

I stared at the open can of beer in her hand. "But…I thought you said your parents were going to be here?"

"Of course that's what I said. That's what we always say when we're throwing a party." Julie laughed. "My parents are vacationing at Hilton Head this weekend. But don't worry, they left a chaperone." She nodded toward the corner, and I followed her gaze. Darryl Potts, her older brother, sat on the recliner.

Darryl was a junior at college. At least, he used to be a junior, before he got kicked out. Supposedly, twelve-year-olds could get better grades in college than he could.

Darryl and Christopher played on the basketball team together my freshman year and ended up becoming very good friends. The only reason I disliked Christopher more than Darryl was because Christopher was the one that got me pregnant. Other than that, they were both equals in asinine behavior.

The house was already starting to fill with people. I could hear even more people in the backyard. The music was blasting in the den—and I had to stop myself from rocking to the beat. This was *not* a party we should have been at.

"Maybe this isn't such a good idea," I said.

Sarah was busy waving at some people on the couch, so I wasn't sure if she even heard me. I tapped her on the shoulder.

"I think we should go," I said.

That got her attention. "Why?"

I looked around quickly before pointing to her stomach. "Babies don't do so well around smoke and alcohol, remember?"

She rolled her eyes. "Stop acting like such a prude," she said. "You used to drink all the time."

I set my jaw. "That was a long time ago. I'm a different person now."

Sarah smiled at me. "I'm not an idiot, Rhonda. I won't go near the alcohol. I'll drink punch all night."

"Sarah…"

"And as long as I don't go outside, I won't be around smoke." She batted her eyes at me. "I only want to stay a few minutes."

"I don't know—"

"Guess who just came in."

I turned to the door to see David walking into the house. I was all smiles, until I saw Christopher strutting in behind him. Johnnie Chang rounded out the bunch.

Before they could take off their coats, they were surrounded by a mob of students. Each of the guys had had a great game that night, and were deserving of all the accolades being heaped upon them. I tried not to notice all of the half-drunk, half-naked girls that were wrapping their arms around David.

I turned back to Sarah, but she had already disappeared. I thought about going to talk to David, but I would have had to fight through the horde just to get near him.

As I inched back against the wall and tried to blend in with the wallpaper, Johnnie Chang broke through the crowd and made his way over to me. Why he was coming my way, I didn't know. I hadn't spoken to him five times that semester.

"Hey, Rhonda," he said. "How's it going?"

Even though Johnnie lived in one of the worst areas of the city (he was one of the few scholarship kids at Piedmont), you couldn't tell by his speech. His family immigrated to America when he was a child, and his parents had made sure that he spoke immaculate English. He didn't even have an accent.

I finally got over the shock of him speaking to me. "I'm okay," I mumbled.

He popped open a can of beer and took a long swig. "Sarah said that you two would probably be coming to the game." He grinned. "You both look pretty good tonight."

I tensed up. Was he trying to pick me up? Had Christopher said something to Johnnie to make him think I was easy?

Before Johnnie could say anything else, someone called to him from across the room. When he turned away, I made my great escape to the kitchen. I had hoped to find Sarah there. Instead, as I entered the room, I bumped into the devil himself.

Christopher stumbled backward a few steps, causing the huge silver crucifix hanging around his neck to bounce against his chest. He looked amused as he downed the rest of the beer in his clear plastic cup.

"Rhonda," Christopher slurred. Although he was an arm's length away from me, I could still feel his hot, alcohol-laced breath as it hit my face. "Darryl said he thought he saw you here." He looked me up and down, and I wanted to immediately take a hot shower. "You look good," he said, stretching three syllables into seven.

"How much have you had to drink tonight?"

He shrugged. "The usual."

Back when we were dating, the "usual" was at minimum three beers. Based on the slur in his voice, he had decided to up his limit.

"Hey, let me grab another beer, and let's talk for a

minute." He winked. "You remember how much we used to *talk* back in the day."

Christopher was trying to get me riled up. And it was working almost too well.

"You're drunk," I said. "Find someone else to harass."

He flashed me a crooked smile. "Do you remember that thing you used to do that I liked so much?" Christopher inched closer. I knew if he took one more step, I was going to kick him in the nuts so hard, he'd be coughing up testosterone all month.

I was praying he would come nearer.

As if on cue, Christopher stumbled closer to me. I planted my right foot and brought my left foot back— ready to kick the field goal of the century. But before I could follow through, David walked up to us.

"Christopher," David said, stepping between us. "A couple of girls are upstairs looking for you."

Christopher looked at me as he talked to David. "How do they look?"

"Does it matter?" he replied.

Christopher grinned and finally peeled his eyes off me. He disappeared from the kitchen, but not before grabbing a beer from the tub on the floor.

I crossed my arms and stared at David. My foot was still cocked and ready to unload, but David had scared away my target.

"Why do you look so mad?" he asked.

"I'm not a helpless girl that needs to be rescued." I finally relaxed my foot. "I can take care of myself."

"I was going for 'thanks,' but I guess that'll have to do."

I had to admit, I was a little flattered that David's protective halo extended from Sarah and included me as well. I didn't want his protection, but I didn't mind his company. Plus, his breath didn't have a hint of alcohol on it. It smelled like mint and white chocolate.

He leaned into me and kicked my sensory glands into overdrive. "If it makes you feel better, I came to rescue Christopher, not you. I can't have you beating up the best player on the basketball team, even if he is an asshole."

"What makes you think I was going to hurt him?"

He tapped his finger lightly on my lips. "You had a scowl on your face worse than anything I've ever seen."

"You can scowl pretty bad as well."

"I know. But if you've noticed, I've been smiling a lot more lately."

I fanned myself. My heart was thumping louder than the music.

"What do you think about the party?" he asked.

I shrugged. "It's great, if you like hanging around guys that just want to grope you and girls that are so drunk they're about to puke on themselves." I sighed. "It's parties like this that remind me why I swore off dating."

"Well, maybe I can change your mind," he said.

"About parties?"

He smiled. "No, about dating."

Damn, he's smooth. I tugged at my sweater and readjusted my glasses. "What are you doing here, anyway? I thought you hated parties."

"I do."

"Then why are you here?"

"Because you're here."

David may not have known it, but it was at that instant I fell in love with him.

He took my hand. "Do you want to dance?"

I nodded. I couldn't have resisted him if I wanted to.

As I followed David into the den, I noticed Sarah out of the corner of my eye, heading toward the kitchen. She flashed me a smile and winked. *Good luck*, she mouthed.

I was grinning too hard to reply back.

David led me to the middle of the room. The song had an up-tempo beat, but neither of us tried to dance too fast. I liked the way he stretched his arms out as he danced, like he was reaching to the sky for divine intervention. We gravitated toward each other—our bodies were close enough for the heat of his skin to jump onto mine. My chest would brush against his every so often. If he didn't mind the contact, I didn't either.

The song ended much too soon, before being replaced with a slow, soulful love song. Both of us lingered in the middle of the floor for a few seconds. I damn sure didn't want to stop dancing. I had forgotten how good it felt.

David reached out and pulled me to him. His arms

wrapped around my body, his hands settled in the small of my back, and he began to sway. My body rocked along with his, like I was an extension of his torso.

I was falling for David—no, I had already fallen for him. I tried to push away the fragments of suspicion and self-doubt that were beginning to pop into my head. I could overanalyze the mess I was getting myself into later. Right now, I just wanted to enjoy the moment.

"That was nice," he said after the song ended.

"Yeah," I whispered back.

He licked his lips as he looked at me. Was this the part where he was going to kiss me?

"I'm thirsty," he said. "You want a soda?"

I sighed and reluctantly nodded. "Actually, I want punch."

"No, you don't," he said. "Not unless you want to drink a cup of Everclear."

I froze. "What? Julie said the punch was alcohol-free."

"I'm sure it was when she originally set it out. Darryl decided to add some kick to it."

I thought about Sarah. She didn't drink soda. If she had gotten thirsty, she would have drunk some of the punch.

"Can you at least taste the alcohol in it?" I asked.

"I doubt it. Darryl probably added enough sugar to cover up any taste. Knowing him, he could have—"

Immediately, I was on the run. I stormed into the kitchen to see Sarah propped against the counter. She was sandwiched between Darryl and Johnnie. A plastic cup dangled in between her fingertips.

I marched over to her and grabbed the cup from her hands. "How much punch have you had tonight?"

"We're having a conversation here, you know," Darryl said.

I ignored him. "Sarah, did you drink any punch tonight?"

"Only a few sips," she said. "Why? It's not like it's alcohol."

By now, David had followed me into the kitchen. "Sarah, what's going on?" he asked.

She shrugged. "I don't know."

I thought about flinging the cup at Darryl, but instead I poured it into the sink. "Why don't you tell Sarah what you put in that punch?"

He sheepishly grinned at us. "Just a little Everclear," he said. "Maybe half a bottle."

As Darryl began to laugh, Sarah's eyes widened like she had just been doused with freezing water. Before I knew it, she was clawing at Darryl's face, as if she was trying to scratch his eyes out.

"You fucking idiot!" she yelled, as Johnnie wrapped his arms around Sarah from behind. She continued to thrash around, trying to get back at Darryl.

"What the hell is wrong with you?" Darryl yelled as he retreated behind David. "It's not like you haven't had a drink before."

Johnnie finally got Sarah's arms pinned to her sides. "Sarah, calm down. I know Everclear's pretty damn strong, but come on. Don't you think you're overreacting?"

Sarah shook her head and finally stopped resisting. She looked at Johnnie for what seemed like hours, and he slowly let her go. Her gaze then bounced from me, to Darryl, and finally settled on David.

"The problem is…I'm pregnant."

chapter[15]
word(problems)

The first few minutes after Sarah's revelation passed by in a flash. David looked like he wanted to punch someone—*anyone*, while Johnnie's face had turned crimson red. Darryl just mumbled an apology and quickly slinked out of the kitchen.

Somehow, we pushed our way through the crowded house and were on our way to Sarah's car before I could blink. In that entire time, we didn't speak a word.

Upon reaching her car, Sarah spent a few seconds rustling through her purse, before finally locating her keys. She tried to stick the key into the lock, but her hand was shaking so much, she ended up scratching the side of the car.

Still not speaking, David walked over to her and took her keys. He unlocked the car and slid into the driver's seat. With her gaze glued to the ground, Sarah circled the car and took the passenger seat. I was barely in the car myself before David started the engine and pulled off.

We were well on our way home when Sarah finally broke the silence.

"Do you think I did any damage? I only took a few sips, I promise. Maybe if I throw up…"

I reached into the front of the car and put my hand on Sarah's shoulder. "It's probably okay."

"Are you sure?"

"Of course." I really wasn't sure, but Sarah didn't need to know that.

Sarah seemed to relax a little. "I'll call the doctor first thing on Monday." She sighed and turned on the radio.

David reached over and snapped it back off.

Sarah just stared at her brother. He looked ahead, only changing his gaze to glance in the side and rearview mirrors.

She lightly touched David's hand, but he shook her off and placed his hand back on the steering wheel.

"David, please say something," Sarah said.

He remained silent.

"David?" she whispered. "Are you mad?"

"How the hell do you think I feel?" He quickly looked

at her, before shaking his head and staring back at the road.

"I wanted to tell you, but I was scared. I wanted—"

"Who the fuck is he?"

Sarah's mouth dropped open. "Is that all you can say?"

David stopped at a red light and turned his gaze on me. "Do you know who did this to her?"

"No," I replied, my voice low.

"Are you lying to me?"

I wanted to sink out of his view. "David, I don't know who the father is."

"Don't yell at Rhonda," Sarah said. "This isn't her fault."

David took a long breath and leaned his head back. "Does Mom know?"

"No."

"When do you plan on telling her?"

Sarah shrugged. "After the baby is born?"

"Not funny." The light turned green and he put the car into motion. "So does this mean you're actually going to have this baby?"

She nodded.

"But you're so young. A baby could ruin your life."

She shook her head. "I'm having this baby."

"But—"

"David, this is my choice, not yours." Sarah was surprisingly calm as she talked to her brother. "I know it's not going to be easy to have this child. But I wouldn't have been able to live with myself if I had ended the pregnancy."

"So you wanted to have a kid?"

"No," she said. "But I'm having one, nevertheless."

David didn't respond to Sarah as he slowed and pulled onto my street. I didn't think I was ever as happy to see home as I was that night.

"You have to tell Mom tomorrow," he said.

Sarah nodded. "I've put it off for long enough. Now that you know, I may as well tell her. It's not like she'll care one way or another."

David parked along the street in front of my house. The lights were off, making the house look almost haunted. But I knew there was at least one soul lurking in the shadows, waiting for me to arrive home.

"Good luck with your mother," I said to Sarah. "Call me if you need me."

"See you on Monday," she said.

I turned to David. He stared back at me like I was a stranger.

"Good night, David." I smiled at him and hoped a flicker of a smile would grace his lips.

David just stared through me, his lips sealed tighter than a crypt. Whatever magic we had shared earlier that night had disappeared.

"How long have you known?" he finally asked.

"Since I began tutoring her."

David slammed his fist into his hand. "You've known for that long? And you didn't tell me?"

I struggled for the right words to say. "It wasn't my place...I didn't think—"

"You'd better go home," he said. Freezing rain was warmer than his voice.

The winter chill stung my eyes as I flung open the car door and ran to the house. I knew things would probably end badly between me and David, but I didn't expect it to end quite so badly or quite so soon.

As I searched my pockets for my keys, I heard footsteps behind me. I turned around, expecting it to be Sarah, coming to console my bruised ego. Instead, David jogged up the driveway and stopped a few feet from me. Maybe he was coming to apologize for acting like such an asshole.

David crossed his arms and stared me down. "Rhonda, I swear, if you know who the guy is that did this to my sister, you'd better tell me."

So much for an apology.

"How many times do I have to say I don't know?" I nodded toward her car. "Ask Sarah. She's the one that's pregnant."

He shook his head. "I can't believe she did this. What was she thinking?" David slammed his fist into his palm again, so hard that he could have broken a few fingers. "After everything I've done for her. After all the time I've spent trying to protect her—"

He sounded so absurd, I couldn't help but laugh.

"David, get over yourself. I promise you, she didn't get pregnant just to spite you or your mother."

"But why wasn't she more careful?"

"People make mistakes."

"Mom is going to have a fit—"

"Sarah doesn't care what her mother thinks. It's *you* she was worried about telling." I stepped closer to him. "Don't you see how important you are to her? Can't you see that she needs you?"

The hard, rigid frown on David's face began to soften. "What am I supposed to do?"

"Stop being her protector and just be her brother."

David sighed. "She could have told me earlier, you know. I would have understood."

I patted his cold cheek. "No, you wouldn't have understood. You would have tried, but you couldn't—you can't—understand what she's going through."

David remained silent for a long time. He looked like he wanted to say something, but his lips couldn't quite form the words. Finally he gave me a half-smile and took my hand in his. He ran his thumb over the back of my hand, and my entire body heated up.

Still smiling, David turned over my hand and softly kissed the inside of my palm. "Thank you," he said. And with that, he turned and ran back to his sister.

I went to unlock the door, but before I could turn the key, the door swung open. Dad wasn't frowning, which was a good thing. However, he wasn't smiling either.

I waved at David and Sarah and watched them drive off. I wasn't ready to speak to Dad yet. I was trying to play back the conversation David and I had just had. If Dad had been standing there for a while, he may have overheard us.

After David and Sarah had driven out of my view, I turned back toward Dad. He was still standing in the doorway. What—did I need a password to come inside? Did I not execute the secret knock correctly?

"How was the party?" he asked. He finally backed up a few steps and allowed me to enter the house.

I shrugged. I didn't want to talk about the party. I hadn't had a chance to sort everything out yet. Besides Sarah's revelation, there was still David and my—well, I didn't even know what to call it. Was it a budding relationship or was it a mistake between two friends? And after Sarah's confession, did we even have a chance at a relationship?

"I heard a car park outside the house," he said. "When I didn't hear the door open, I decided to come see what was going on."

I nodded. "Sorry, I was just talking—"

"Who's the boy?"

I sighed. "David Gamble, Sarah's brother."

Dad scrunched up his face and began to rub his jaw. I could tell he couldn't quite place the name. He knew he had heard it before somewhere.

I thought about not telling Dad anything else about David and just disappearing to my room. But I was tired of all the half-truths I had been concocting about Sarah and David. If Sarah could come clean, so could I.

"He plays on the basketball team. The shooting guard." I could have recited more information. The jersey number. The number of points, rebounds, assists, and steals he amassed during the game. The number of times he kissed me (in my dreams). But by the look on Dad's face, he didn't need any more information.

Dad went to the pantry and pulled out a bag of potato chips. "I thought you were going to the party with Sarah." He shoved a handful of chips into his mouth and sat at the table. "Why didn't you tell me about this boy going to the party with y'all as well?"

I sat down across from Dad. "I didn't know he was going to the party. He showed up after the game."

"Are y'all friends?"

I nodded. He crunched on his chips.

"Are y'all...more than friends?"

I wished I knew.

I shrugged. "I've gotten to know him better as I've been tutoring Sarah."

Dad shook his head. "I don't like this."

I was tempted to grab a pint of ice cream from the freezer. I didn't know if I was going to make it through the night without it.

"I'm eighteen years old," I said. "I should be dating."

I could hardly believe what I was saying. Maybe David *had* changed my opinion on dating.

"But he plays on the same team as that other punk." Dad refused to call Christopher by his name. "He's trying to use you."

"*Use* me?"

"Come on," he said. "You're smart. You have to realize that guys talk. That Gamble boy probably thinks he can—that you'll give him whatever he wants."

I thought back to the way Johnnie had approached me at the party. "David isn't like that."

"Didn't you say the same thing about the other boy?"

That shut me up real quick.

"I should have said something to him at the basketball game," Dad continued. "That boy needs to be taken down a notch."

"Why did you want to talk to David?"

"Not him," Dad muttered. "The other punk."

I frowned. "Dad, you told me you wouldn't say anything to Christopher or his father."

"But it's not right," he said. "He deserves to be punished."

I shook my head. "You promised, remember?"

Dad grimaced, but nodded. "I remember."

Christopher was an asshole, but his father was one hundred times worse. Christopher had a hard time staying out of trouble, and his father didn't have any qualms over using extreme discipline to force him back onto the straight and narrow path. As much as I hated Christopher, no one deserved punishment like that. Not even him.

When I finally agreed to terminate the pregnancy, I made Dad promise not to say anything to Christopher or his father. I told Dad that getting the McCulloughs involved would drag the situation out in the open, and that I just wanted to get it over with. Dad didn't like it, but he agreed. So that following weekend, while Christopher went on a church retreat with his youth group, I headed to Atlanta.

Dad rose from the table, his chips still in his hands. "Is there anything else about your new friends I should know?"

I rubbed the back of my neck and looked down at the table. "Sarah's pregnant."

"Why am I not surprised?" Dad gave off a condescending laugh. "You'd think you high school kids would learn from each other's mistakes."

My stomach lurched. "That's a mean thing to say."

"No, it's a cold and hard truth." He started toward his bedroom, but stopped at the edge of the kitchen. He passed his bag of chips back and forth from one hand to another.

"Well, is she going to have an…"

I didn't reply. I just watched Dad struggle with the words he couldn't bring himself to say.

He cleared his throat. "Is she going to end the pregnancy?"

I narrowed my eyes and glared at my father. "No, she isn't getting an *abortion*."

Dad's gaze immediately shifted off me. I had said the

forbidden word. The A-word. The word we had danced around for the past three years. The word that had ripped us apart.

Dad finally looked back at me. For a few seconds, his eyes were vulnerable. His mouth dropped slightly open, and he shuffled a half-step toward me.

"Rhonda…"

I stood up and inched toward him. Something in his voice caught me off-guard. Hearing him speak my name like that made me feel like I was teetering on the edge of a waterfall.

"Dad?"

Dad shook his head, and his eyes returned to their cool and impassive state. "It's getting late," he said, his voice gruff. "We'll talk about this more in the morning."

I sighed as Dad left the room. I should have known better than to hope for a meaningful conversation with my father. Dad refused to talk about my pregnancy and abortion. He had tried many times before, but just like tonight, he could never find the words.

chapter[16]
reductio ad(absurdum)

Sarah's pregnancy was the main topic of discussion on Monday morning at school. While I'd like to think that Piedmont Academy was fairly progressive, Sarah's pregnancy was a *big* deal. Like me, I was sure there were plenty of girls that had gotten pregnant while in high school, but Sarah was the first girl that actually planned to carry the pregnancy to term.

Sarah wasn't the only one being dragged through the rumor mill. Because of my theatrics at the party, my name was being thrown around as well. It was just like it had been when Christopher dumped me. Groups of students would turn silent as I neared them, only to erupt into a fit of giggles as soon as I passed. I could feel hundreds of eyes on me as I made my way down the hallways. It was a strange feeling—going from being popular during my freshman year, to being a nobody, to suddenly becoming famous again. No, not famous—*infamous.*

I had the chance to talk to Sarah briefly, right before my English class. Sarah had abandoned her usual glamorous look—no lipstick, no eye shadow, no fancy jewelry. She looked naked.

I waved her over. A large smile came to her face once she saw me, and she made her way through the horde of students in the hallway to me. Actually, it wasn't that tough for her to navigate through the dense hallways. The student body looked to be avoiding her like she was diseased.

"How did it go last night?" I asked.

"I'll have to tell you later," she said. "Right now, I've got to go to the guidance counselor's office. Supposedly, there are some 'issues' she wants to discuss." Sarah tilted her head to the side and rubbed her chin. "Hmm, I wonder what that could be about."

"Maybe you should go home."

"And listen to Mom bitch all day? I'm better off at school."

I tried to ignore a group of freshmen girls as they passed by. They stared at us as if we were animals in a cage.

Sarah quickly glanced at the students and took a few

steps back from me. "I'd better get out of here," she said, looking away from my face.

"Sarah, what's wrong?"

She shook her head quickly. "Nothing."

Another group of students walked past, whispering loudly enough for us to know they were talking about us. Sarah stared at a poster on the wall.

"I'm really sorry about all of this," she mumbled. "Hopefully, they'll stop talking about you in a few days."

"They'll stop talking about *us* in a few days."

Sarah just shrugged, and headed down the hallway.

By the time lunch came around, rumors had started to spread about who the father was. Some folks speculated that it was a teacher. Others were malicious enough to say it could have been any one of the football players, being that she slept with *all* of them. One pervert was vile enough to suggest that Sarah was carrying her and my love child. If he didn't sound like such an idiot, I would have punched him.

Murmurs and whispers rippled throughout the cafeteria as Sarah made her way from the lunch line. She quickly glanced at her usual table. Her friends were too busy staring at their empty trays to look at her. Of course, she couldn't have sat at that table if she wanted to. Someone had already taken her seat.

Sarah could have sat with me, but I knew she wouldn't. She was trying to contain the damage.

Sarah found an empty seat in the corner of the room

opposite from us. She sat with a bunch of students that didn't even look in her direction. She just slowly picked at her food, all the while keeping her face glued to the table.

I wished I could have said my friends were more supportive of Sarah, but even they were taking part in the rumor mill.

"I can't believe she's pregnant," Xavier said. "Who's the father?"

I shrugged.

Xavier leaned closer to me. "Is it true—"

"No."

"But—"

"Xavier, if you don't shut up, I'm going to shove my lunch tray down your throat."

"Don't get mad at Xavier," Gail said. "It isn't his fault your friend got pregnant."

I shook my head. "How can you guys be so mean?"

Gail crossed her arms. "The way I see it, if you do the crime, you have to do the time."

I glared at Gail. "Don't be such a bitch." I began to rise from the table. "I'm going to get Sarah."

Gail grabbed my arm and yanked me back to my seat. "Are you crazy? Why are you going to bring her over here?"

"She shouldn't have to eat by herself."

Gail pulled me closer to her. "She got herself into this mess," she said. "She even dragged you into it. Do you hear what people are saying about you?"

I pried Gail's fingers away from my wrist. "I don't care."

"But what about flying under the radar?" she asked. "You shouldn't bring that much attention to yourself."

"Why? Because I'm smart? Because I'm black?"

She looked away from me.

"Oh, I know. Because I'm fat."

Gail cleared her throat. "High school kids can be vicious."

"I know," I said. "I'm listening to one now."

I didn't wait around to hear if Gail was going to say anything else. I stood up, and immediately every eye in the cafeteria was on me.

My legs felt like they were made of twigs. My stomach felt like it was trying to digest a rotten egg. I quickly glanced at Gail and Xavier. They were probably the only ones in the cafeteria not looking at me. So much for my friends.

I slung my bookbag over my shoulder, picked up my tray, and walked to Sarah's table. I tried to ignore the eyes glued to my back, and focused on placing one foot in front of the other. Thirty-three steps later, I stood in front of Sarah.

I sat down, and we spent the next five minutes nibbling on our food in cautious silence. It was like we were in a play—the entire cafeteria was our audience, and we had both caught a bad case of stage fright.

"Why aren't you sitting with your friends?" she finally asked.

"I *am* sitting with my friend."

Sarah smiled. "Thanks, but I think those guys behind you may have a different opinion."

I turned around. Both Gail and Xavier stood behind me, holding their half-empty lunch trays.

"Do you have a couple of extra seats?" Gail asked. "We seemed to have lost ours, and our food is getting cold."

I laughed. "You're eating a chef salad. It was already cold."

Gail smiled a reply and sat down beside me. Xavier slipped around the table and sat beside Sarah.

Xavier leaned closer to Sarah. "I'm kinda seeing someone right now, but if you're ever looking for a boyfriend…"

Sarah let out a loud and deep laugh. It was probably the first time she had laughed all day. She paused long enough to lean over and give Xavier a quick peck on the cheek. It wasn't anything major—even with all the scrutiny we were under, I was sure no one saw it.

He shrugged, his face crimson. "Pregnant or not, she's still gorgeous."

∴

During lunch, Sarah filled me in on what happened after she told her mother about her pregnancy. By the time the shouting match had ended, they had shattered four plates, thrown three books, and broken the hinges off Sarah's bedroom door.

Against my better judgment, I agreed to stop by Sarah's

house after tutoring. Sarah had a test tomorrow, and I was going to quiz her on her trig functions. Plus, I was dying to see David. I had been hoping to talk to him at school, but I didn't see him. However, with the extra attention on all of us, I didn't think it was a good idea to talk to him at school, anyway.

I pulled into the Gambles' driveway, ready to throw myself into the wonderful world of trigonometry. But as Sarah opened the door, it looked like hyperbolic functions were the furthest thing from her mind.

"I shouldn't have asked you to come by," Sarah said after I entered the house. "For some reason, my mother wants to talk to you."

I frowned. "What does she want with me?"

"I wish I knew," she said. "All I know is, she wants to talk to you. In private."

I grabbed Sarah by the shoulders. "What did you tell her?"

Her voice sounded like it had been pulled through a cheese grate. "She knows you were the one that took me to the clinic."

I had a mini-heart attack. "Is she upset?"

"You'll have to ask her yourself. As soon as I told her about the trip to Atlanta, she kicked me out of her office and instructed me to send you up there once you arrived." Sarah pointed up the stairs. "It's second door on the right. You'd better not keep her waiting."

I headed up the stairs. With each step I took, I felt like

I was on a death march. I paused at the top of the staircase and looked back down at Sarah. She sat at the bottom of the stairs, her arms folded across her body.

I continued down the hallway until I got to Ms. Gamble's office. The door was slightly ajar. Ms. Gamble sat at her desk, her eyes focused on the paperwork in front of her. The entire room was shielded in black, except for the light exuding from a small desk lamp.

I knocked softly on the door and pushed it open. "Ms. Gamble?"

She looked up from her desk, her reading glasses perched on her nose. "Rhonda, come on in. I've been expecting you."

I crept into the room and stood as far away from her as I could.

Ms. Gamble flipped a switch on her desk, immediately basking the room in bright white light. "Please, have a seat," she said. "And close the door behind you."

I shut the door and shuffled to one of the chairs in front of the desk. The desk looked like it belonged in some CEO's office. It was large and sturdy, with intricate Greek lettering carved into its legs.

The room looked more like a library than an office. Huge wooden bookshelves lined three of the walls, and each bookshelf was filled to the brim. The fourth wall, directly behind the desk, displayed her two diplomas, as well as various awards and citations. As my eyes adjusted to the light, I could just make out *summa cum laude* on her diploma from Georgia Tech.

"I'm sure Sarah has told you how disappointed I am in her." Ms. Gamble reclined in her chair and peered at me. "I expected Sarah to get a quality education at Piedmont, not to end up pregnant."

"It was a mistake," I uttered.

Ms. Gamble burst into laughter. "I would hope so. I'd hate to think my daughter got impregnated on purpose."

I looked down at my feet and tried to disappear into the fabric of the chair.

"Well, has she at least told you who the father is?"

"No, ma'am."

"Knowing Sarah, there's no telling who the little bastard is," she said. "But it doesn't really matter. Once she has an abortion, this will all be over."

I lurched forward. "She's getting the abortion?"

"Of course she is," Ms. Gamble said. "What other option does she have?"

"But half the school already knows she's pregnant."

Ms. Gamble shrugged. "We could say that she only *thought* she was pregnant. Or better yet, maybe she was just lying to get some boy's attention." Ms. Gamble chuckled. "You know my daughter well enough to know that it isn't beyond reason to think she would make something like this up. She loves the spotlight."

"But what if someone finds out—"

"Let me worry about that," she said, before smiling.

"Sarah told me about the little stunt you two pulled, using her cousin's ID to try to schedule an abortion. I'll give Sarah this much—it was very ingenious of her. Maybe she has some moxie after all." Ms. Gamble leaned across her desk. "I could understand Sarah backing out at the last minute. I'm just curious why you didn't try harder to talk her into getting the procedure."

"I was only there for support. I wasn't there to talk her into anything."

"But weren't you?" she asked. "I know more about you than you think. I know you were a patient at that same clinic three years ago." She slid her glasses off her face. "Like I said before, I believe in doing my homework."

"But how—"

"Don't worry, Sarah didn't tell me." She smirked. "You'd be surprised at the level of file access a Supreme Court Justice can get."

I sighed. At least Sarah hadn't been the one to reveal my secret, although I'm sure she wanted to. It was turning out that she was tougher than either her mother or I imagined.

"I'm going to tell you something that not even my ex-husband knows," she said, rising from the desk. She walked behind her chair and dug her fingers into the brown leather. "Just like you, I once found myself in the unfortunate situation of being young, dumb, and pregnant."

For some reason, my gaze fell from her face to her stomach, like I was looking for proof.

"I even had you beat by a year," she said as she gazed at her law degree. "I was fourteen." She turned to me. "My uncle did it."

Instinctively, I brought my hand to my mouth. "I'm sorry."

"Looking back, it was one of the best things that could have happened to me. It made me stronger. More determined. I was not going to be another young girl stuck in Darlington County for the rest of my life. I had plans. I had a future. And no one was going stop me from obtaining my goals."

"So you had the abortion."

"Yes, and now I'm a State Supreme Court justice." Ms. Gamble narrowed her eyes at me. "Rhonda, my daughter isn't like us. She isn't focused. She isn't motivated. But I still believe in her. I know she can succeed. We both know she's capable of it." She shook her head. "But she can't succeed if she's got a newborn baby weighing her down. Wouldn't you agree?"

Against my will, I felt myself nodding.

"I've threatened Sarah in every way possible. I've even promised to throw her out if she decides to have this baby," she said. "But the girl has too much of her father in her. She's stubborn and unpractical."

I wasn't sure, but I thought I saw tears collecting in the corners of Ms. Gamble's eyes.

"You're her friend," she said. "You can talk some sense

into her. You can convince her that she needs to have this abortion."

It seemed like a two-ton weight was sitting squarely on my chest. "I'm sorry, but it's not my place to tell her what to do."

"Yes, it is," she said. "We have to help those who can't help themselves, Rhonda. We have to be strong for Sarah." She nodded toward her diplomas. "Did you know the president of Georgia Tech and I were classmates? I have lunch with him every time I'm in Atlanta."

The weight on my chest seemed to increase. "What are you implying?"

"Whether Sarah believes it or not, I love her and I will do everything in my power to help her succeed in life," she said. "I also believe in playing fair, but not when it comes to my children." She circled her desk and extended her hand to me. "Can I count on your help?"

I took a deep breath and tried to calm down. It seemed like the entire room was spinning. How could this be happening? Was Ms. Gamble really saying what I thought she was saying? I thought about all the ways I could persuade Sarah to have the abortion. Maybe if I talked to her again. Maybe if I explained the ramifications. Maybe if—

Suddenly, I stopped with all of the hypothesizing and laughed to myself. I didn't know why I was even stressing about what to tell Ms. Gamble. I really only had one option.

I looked at Ms. Gamble's Georgia Tech diploma once

more, and slowly rose from my chair. "I'm sorry," I said, my knees wobbling under me. "Sarah has made her decision."

Ms. Gamble eyed me silently for a few seconds, before shaking my hand. "I hear that USC has a very challenging engineering program. I hope you enjoy it."

She released my hand and headed back toward her chair. "Please close the door on your way out."

My legs felt like Jell-O as I exited the room and headed down the stairs. The past few minutes almost felt like a nightmare. Was Ms. Gamble serious? Did I really just throw away the best chance I had at getting a scholarship from Tech?

"How did it go?" Sarah asked as I neared the base of the staircase. She was gripping the banister hard enough to leave indentations of her fingertips. "Is everything okay?"

"Why didn't you have the abortion?" I asked. "What made you change your mind?"

Sarah leaned against the banister. "To be honest, I'm not really sure. I guess it was for a lot of different reasons." She frowned. "Why do you ask?"

"I just want you to be sure—"

"I'm positive." Sarah looked me directly in the face. "I'm not having an abortion."

Suddenly, my legs felt like they were made of steel. "That's what I thought." I smiled as I started off toward the kitchen. "Come on. We've got a trig exam to study for."

chapter[17]
the absolute value of(0)

I had been sitting in silence at my kitchen table for twenty-five minutes, unable to move, my gaze glued to the rectangular temptress lying before me. I had managed to estimate its approximate surface area, perimeter, and weight (39.19 square inches, 2.3 feet, 1.7 ounces). I had even picked it up once, and then immediately placed it back on the table.

I was staring so hard at the envelope, I didn't even notice Dad unlock the door and walk into the house until he flipped on the lights. "Why are you sitting in the dark?"

"Just thinking."

He walked toward the table but stopped upon seeing the letter. "Georgia Tech?"

I nodded. "It's from the scholarship office."

Dad placed his briefcase on the table and reached for the letter. "Why don't you let me open—"

"No!" I jumped up and snatched the letter from the table. I dropped back to my seat, the envelope pressed against my chest. "I'll open it," I said, my voice calmer.

I closed my eyes, offered up a quick prayer, and slowly opened the envelope.

I felt my entire body sink as I read the first paragraph of the letter.

Dad rounded the table and stood beside me. "Well?"

I stifled the tears that were begging to be released. "I'm on the waiting list for the scholarship."

"That's great!"

I cut my eyes toward my father. "What's great about that?"

He gingerly placed his hand on my shoulder. "That means you're still in the running. They could have just turned you down completely." He smiled. "All you have to do is wait for a few people to decline the scholarship."

"Why would anyone turn down a scholarship to Georgia Tech?"

Dad sat down beside me. "Maybe this is a sign that you should stay closer to home," he began. "I know you really had your heart set on Georgia Tech, but I have a friend in the civil engineering department at USC that—"

I slammed my fist on the table. "Who said I wanted

to stay close to home? Who said I even wanted to major in civil engineering?"

Dad frowned. "I just assumed—"

"I don't need your help," I said, turning away from him. "I'm old enough to make the decision for myself."

"Well, you're not acting like it." Dad rose from the table. "I don't know what's gotten into you lately. You never used to be so disrespectful." He reached into his pocket and dropped a few bills on the table. "Why don't you order yourself some Chinese food. Maybe that'll cheer you up."

Yeah, like a couple of fried egg rolls would solve all of my problems. I scooped the money from the table. "What do you want me to order for you? Moo Goo Gai Pan?"

He shook his head as he headed down the hallway. "Nothing for me," he said. "Jackie and I had an early dinner at Antonio's."

Just fucking great. Dad and the Teeny Bopper have dinner at a fancy Italian restaurant, and I'm stuck eating dinner out of a paper carton.

I placed the order, slumped into my chair, and thought back to my conversation with Ms. Gamble. I had no way of knowing if she ever acted on her threat. I guess at this point, it didn't matter. Sarah was having her baby, and more than likely, I was going to USC.

I thought about calling Gail or Sarah for encouragement, but instead found my finger hitting the redial button.

"China Palace. How may I help you?" someone chimed on the other end of the phone. God, was everyone having a good day except for me?

"This is Rhonda Lee. I just placed an order about five minutes ago," I said, looking at the menu through blurred eyes. "I need to cancel my order."

"I'm sorry to hear that," he said, although he didn't sound the least bit sorry. "Was there a problem with our service?"

"No problem. I'm just not in the mood for Chinese food." A solitary tear splashed against the menu. "I think tonight is more of a 'vanilla ice cream and chocolate cake' type of evening."

∴

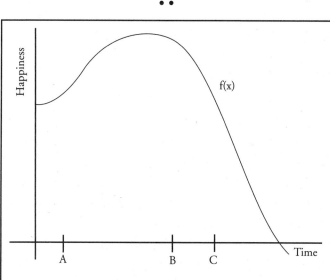

f(x) = Happiness due to scholarship, in relation to time (x) where,

x = A ≡ date I received initial letter from Georgia Tech

x = B ≡ date I "discussed" Sarah's options with her mother

x = C ≡ date I was put on the goddamn waiting list

I was still in a shitty mood a week after I received the letter.

Gail, Sarah, and Xavier did their best to console my bruised ego, but I wasn't interested in "looking on the bright side of things." I hadn't taken the SAT four times and kept a straight-A average just to get put on a waiting list.

The one person that could cheer me up was too busy with basketball practices to offer his condolences. So much for thinking there had been a spark between David and me.

I was so upset, I found myself snapping at a few of my students at the community center. Bryce even sent me home early one day, saying that maybe I needed a little vacation.

I didn't need a damn vacation. I needed a full scholarship to Georgia Tech.

I woke up on Monday morning fully intending to spray venom at anyone that dared approach me. I got dressed, forced a couple of burnt pieces of toast down my throat, and stormed out of the house. And then, something caught my eye, causing me to momentarily lose my scowl.

Three red long-stemmed roses lay against my hood.

I quickly looked around as I walked to the car. I picked up the roses and brought them to my nose. They smelled like they had just been pulled from a garden. Whoever had placed them on my car had left them there this morning.

I frowned as I looked back at the house. Did Dad leave them for me? He knew I loved roses (not that he ever gave them to me). He was already gone by the time I woke up, so it was possible that he left the roses. Maybe he finally noticed I had been stomping around the house for the past few days.

Walking a lot softer, I went back into the house and dropped the roses into an empty vase. I sniffed them once more, and I headed back to my car. I didn't realize I was smiling until I was halfway to school.

I had almost forgotten about the roses until I sat down at lunch. Xavier was working on a newspaper article, so it was just Gail and Sarah today. As I bit into my sandwich, I caught Sarah staring at me, with a grin on her face that could rival a circus clown.

I dropped my sandwich. "It was you, wasn't it?"

That made her grin even more. "Nope, it wasn't me."

Gail looked up from her textbook. "What are y'all talking about?"

"Someone left three roses on my car this morning. I thought Dad left them, until Sarah started beaming at me."

Sarah faked a look of shock. "I promise, it wasn't me. I had nothing to do with it." She winked. "All I did was give him the name of a florist."

"You gave the name of a florist to my father?"

"Your father?" Sarah rolled her eyes. "Don't you realize today is Valentine's Day?"

Valentine's Day? I was so busy being angry, I didn't even realize it was February 14th. I shook my head. "So it wasn't my father? Then who—"

Suddenly, a heart-shaped light bulb switched on in my head.

"You should have heard him," Sarah said. "He was on the phone for fifteen minutes, trying to pick the right type of flower to get you."

I felt the corners of my mouth reach to my earlobes. "He was?"

Sarah leaned over the table. "He was so nervous, he spilled orange juice all over his shirt this morning."

Gail cleared her throat, and Sarah and I stopped grinning at each other. "What in the world are you two talking about?"

"Haven't you been paying attention?" Sarah asked. "David bought Rhonda three long-stem roses." She turned back to me. "Please tell me they were red roses."

My smile reemerged. "They were red."

Sarah squealed and clasped her hands together. "You guys are gonna make such a great couple."

I finally forced my mouth into a straight line. "Wait a minute, who said anything about us being a couple?"

"Come on, Rhonda. The boy brought you red roses on Valentine's Day. That means he likes you." Sarah shook her head. "What the hell are they teaching you guys in those advanced classes?"

I thought back to the roses sitting on my nightstand. "I don't know. I'm not really looking for a relationship."

"Rhonda, you can't even say his name without turning

three shades of purple," Sarah said. "Just admit it. You like him."

I looked at Gail. "What do you think?"

Gail frowned. "You don't want to know."

Sarah sighed. "Why do you always have to be so damn negative? Don't you want Rhonda to be happy?"

Gail looked like she wanted to pummel Sarah. "That's easy for you to say," she said to Sarah. "But what happens if David breaks up with her? Will she be happy then?" Gail shot her laser-beam gaze into me. "Or maybe you've forgotten how things ended with Christopher."

It was amazing how a person could go from the highest of highs to the lowest of lows in a matter of seconds. I tried to scrape my bruised ego off the ground. "David's not like Christopher."

"Of course he is," Gail replied. "And all they want is sex."

"That's not true," Sarah said.

Gail laughed sarcastically. "Says the girl that's four months pregnant."

Just like I had moments earlier, Sarah came crashing back down to Earth.

"You know, it's pretty damn convenient for you to have a boyfriend, when you're so hell-bent on ruining other people's relationships." Sarah narrowed her eyes at Gail. "You're not that different than me and Rhonda. Given the right circumstances, you could have been the pregnant one."

Gail snorted. "Wanna bet?"

Sarah slapped her hand against her forehead and looked

at me. "How do you stay friends with her? She is the most arrogant, self-righteous person I have ever met."

I shrugged. "Believe me, it takes a lot of practice."

Gail rolled her eyes and huffed in reply.

"Rhonda likes David, and David likes Rhonda," Sarah continued. "Who cares if they sleep together or not? Haven't you heard of birth control?"

"No birth control is one-hundred percent effective," Gail said as if she was reading from a textbook. "She could still get pregnant. And don't get me started on sexually transmitted diseases."

"She could also get hit by a bus as she walked across the street," Sarah said. "If she loves him—"

"Love? Who cares about love?" Gail sighed. "Rhonda, why are you even putting yourself in this situation? This time next year, you're going to be in college. Even if things work out with David—and I seriously doubt they will—is it worth starting a relationship that's destined to be over by the end of the summer?"

I puffed up my chest. "I think it is."

"Of course it is," Sarah gushed. "You and David can make a long-distance relationship work."

Gail crossed her arms. "And just where are *you* going to be next year after graduation, Sarah?"

I wasn't going to let Gail beat up on Sarah anymore. "Gail, that's enough—"

"No, it's okay," Sarah said. "Gail's right. I'll be here,

raising my child. Maybe I'll go to one of the local schools part-time, after the baby gets bigger."

Gail glanced at me. "That's a long time to put your life on hold for a bad case of infatuation."

These girls were starting to give me a headache. "Just because I date David doesn't mean I'll sleep with him."

"You can't honestly believe that." Gail nodded toward Sarah's old table. "Sarah, didn't your brother go out with Stacy Hayes last year?"

Sarah slowly nodded.

"For how long?" Gail continued.

"Maybe a week or two," Sarah said.

"And did he sleep with her?"

"How am I supposed to know—"

Gail planted her fists on the table. "Did he fuck her or not?"

Sarah frowned. "Yes."

Gail turned to me with a triumphant look on her face. "He slept with her, and then he dropped her."

Sarah shook her head. "I didn't say—"

"You didn't have to say it." Gail continued to stare at me. "Rhonda, do you really want the same thing to happen to you?"

"Of course not," I said. "But it won't happen to me."

"How do you know?" Gail asked.

"Because it happened to me already."

Gail looked at me, but didn't reply. Maybe she had finally run out of words.

"Thanks for the advice," I said, "but I don't think either one of you is qualified to give me pointers on my love life."

Sarah smiled. "That's probably the smartest thing I've heard all lunch period."

∴

David was leaning against my car as I walked out of the school building. He looked so...perfect. God, I wanted him to *be* perfect. Was that too much to ask for?

"Did you like the roses?" he asked as I neared the car.

"They were beautiful."

David smiled. "I hoped you would like them. I wanted to get a card as well, but I couldn't find—"

"We need to talk."

David's smile disappeared. Maybe he could hear the concern in my voice.

I planted myself in front of him. "You know Christopher and I used to date."

He nodded.

"What else do you know?"

David looked out toward the football field, before turning back to me. "He dumped you."

"And...?"

"That's it. Why, is there more?"

"I slept with him. I lost my virginity to him."

David's gaze darted away from me before I had finished my statement. "I'm not surprised, but that's not information I need to know."

"I want you to know," I said. I wanted to tell him more, about how Christopher had gotten me pregnant and how he wasn't man enough to own up to his actions and how I was forced to have an abortion and how much it hurt…but I didn't.

"I know you used to date Stacy Hayes. The rumor is that it only took you a week to get her pants off."

"Since when did you start paying attention to gossip?"

"I have to pay attention when it concerns someone I really like." I dumped my bookbag on top of the hood. "I heard you slept with her, and then broke up with her the following week. Is that true?"

David's silence was answer enough.

I balled my hands and stuffed them in my pockets. "You're disgusting."

"Listen, it wasn't like that. Yeah, we broke up, but it wasn't because I slept with her."

I rolled my eyes. "Let's not waste each other's time. If you're just getting with me for easy sex, we can end this now."

"What?" David shuffled backwards a few steps. "Who said anything about sex? Can't we at least try a date first?"

"But don't you want to have sex?"

"Of course I do." He shrugged. "What high school senior doesn't want to?"

If I had had the roses with me, I would have flung them

in his face. "I should have known Gail was right," I muttered. "You're all alike."

"What are you talking about?" David asked. "Don't beat me up for being honest with you. Isn't that what you want?"

I paused, and quickly nodded.

"Like I was saying before, I'd be lying if I said I didn't want to have sex *eventually*. But eventually is a long time away."

"But you and Stacy—"

"That was a mistake. A lapse in judgment. You can't hold that against me."

He was right, *I* couldn't. *I* had made far worse decisions.

"What's got you so uptight?" He inched toward me and took my hand in his. "What's wrong?"

"It's been a long time since I was in a relationship." I said, staring at the cracked blacktop. "I just don't want to get screwed over."

"I won't do that to you. We'll take things slow."

"How slow? You won't get...frustrated?"

David winked. "I'll find another way to relieve stress."

He was saying the same things Christopher would have said, but for some reason I believed him. Was I being a fool? Was I walking into a trap?

Was it worth the risk?

I finally allowed myself to smile. "I really did like the roses."

David smiled back. "I'm glad you liked them, Rhonda the Rhombus."

I burst into laughter. "You're not ever going to let me forget that, are you?"

"Of course not." He slightly squeezed my hand before releasing it. "I'd better get to practice. I'm already late." He began to backpedal toward the school. "I'll call you tonight, okay?"

I nodded, and watched him scamper off toward the gym.

As I grabbed my books and slid into my car, I could feel my entire body tingling. Part of me (okay, all of me) had wanted David to reach out, wrap his arms around me, and plant one of those magical kisses on my lips. If the world was like geometry, he would be a perfect circle, and I'd be a big, fat…rhombus.

But maybe, just maybe, rhombuses needed love too.

chapter[18]
integration by(parts)

"Oh my God!" I yelled. "Did you see that shot?"

David and I were watching the Duke-UNC game. Well, we were watching it, but not together. He sat in his house and I sat in mine. The phone was cradled against my neck, in the same position it had been in every night for the past week.

"I can't believe he made that shot," David moaned. His beloved Blue Devils were down by ten points with less than a minute left.

"Come on," I said. "Admit it. That was a great shot. Legendary, even."

"Let's not get carried away. It isn't like a championship is on the line. The NCAA tournament hasn't even started yet."

"Are you kidding?" I could hear my voice rising. "When's the last time you've seen a shot like that? That was almost as good as Jordan's jumper over Bryon Russell to win the '98 NBA championship."

David snorted. "I'm sorry. I didn't realize Jordan was allowed to push his defender to the floor in order to get an open shot."

"Russell didn't get pushed down. He slipped."

"He was fouled."

"He lost his footing."

"He—"

"Do you really want to argue about this?" I asked as my mouth curled into a smile. "Or have you forgotten about all the other arguments you lost this week."

David was quiet for a second, before he started laughing. "See, that's what I like about you," he said. "You're smart, you're cute, and you know almost as much about basketball as I do."

"Actually, I probably know more about basketball than you do," I replied. "I just don't want to show off."

He laughed again. "The sad thing is, you're probably right about that, too."

The game went to commercial, and I turned down the television volume. I looked at the unopened textbook in my lap. "I really need to get off the phone. I haven't gotten a lick of homework done."

"Yeah, I have a bunch of homework to do as well," he replied.

Then we proceeded to spend twenty more minutes talking about basketball.

Finally, David conceded defeat on his argument that Magic Johnson's Lakers were a better team than Jordan's Bulls. "Okay, for real, I'm getting off the phone," he said. "Will you be coming by the house this weekend?"

"I don't think so. Sarah doesn't have any math exams coming up for a while, and she's at the point where she hardly needs my help with her homework."

There was a long pause on the other end of the phone. "That's too bad," he finally said. "I was really looking forward to seeing you this weekend."

I curled the phone cord around my finger. The batteries had long ago died out in my cordless phone. "Just because I'm not tutoring Sarah doesn't mean we can't see each other this weekend. We can always go to the movies or something."

"You mean like on a date? But I thought you wanted to take things slow."

I laughed. "I meant *slow* as in I don't want you trying to shove your hands up my shirt," I said. "I think I'll be safe at the movies."

"To be honest, I'm glad you said something about going out. I've been dying to see you outside of my house, and in a setting that doesn't involve homework," he said. "We can even invite Sarah or Gail along, if you want."

David's offer was very chivalrous, but truthfully, I had no desire to share him with Sarah or Gail or anyone else.

Before David and I hung up, we decided which movie we wanted to see. We even picked the theater and discussed what type of snacks we liked.

Now all I had to do was get permission from my father.

I tiptoed to the living room. Dad sat on the couch, his fingers wrapped around a Coke bottle. Sports highlights flashed across the television screen.

"You were on the phone for quite a while," he said. "The Gamble girl must really need a lot of help with her homework."

I just smiled and nodded. Due to the beauty of caller ID, Dad thought that because the Gamble name was popping up on the display, I must have been spending all my time talking to Sarah.

I cleared my throat. "Can I go out on Friday night?"

Dad didn't turn away from the television. "With who? Gail and Xavier?"

I inched closer to the door and smiled the most innocent smile that I could muster. "Actually, with David."

Dad slowly turned to me. If looks could kill, it would have been a death by visual bludgeoning.

"I'll let you think about it," I said as I backed out of the room. "We'll talk about it tomorrow."

I could hear Dad shuffling toward the kitchen as

I headed to my room. I could have stayed in the living room and debated all night long the reasons that I should be able to go out with David. But I didn't want to argue. I didn't want to fight. For once, I wanted Dad to treat me like a normal teenage girl and give me permission to go out on a date. I was eighteen, and he needed to respect my choices.

Plus, it was a hell of a lot easier to walk out of the front door than climb out of my bedroom window.

The next morning, Dad emerged from his room looking like he spent the night fighting a grizzly bear. He flipped on the coffee maker, scratched his backside, and finally turned to me.

"We're having a family dinner this weekend," he said. "Invite the boy over. If I find him acceptable, you can go out with him."

If I find him acceptable? Dad made David sound like a cut of meat.

I agreed, and Dad filled me in on the details of the evening. It turned out that Dad had consulted Jackie for advice on my dating request. Jackie suggested that we all—me, Dad, David and her—get together for dinner. She thought it would be a good way for all of us to "bond."

If Jackie had her way, she would have probably orchestrated many more family dinners. She and Dad were getting awfully close. The six-month marker had come and gone, and she was still around. Dad really seemed to like her, and I couldn't figure out why. She wasn't anything like Mom. And maybe Dad could replace Mom, but I never would.

∴

On the night of our highly anticipated (or more like highly dreaded) dinner, Jackie looked less like a teacher and more like a girlfriend as she maneuvered around the kitchen, throwing things into pots and chopping up vegetables. Her hair was long and flowing, with freshly dyed highlights. She wasn't wearing her glasses, either. She must have caught me staring at her, because she smiled and pointed to her eyes.

"I got contacts."

"They look nice," I mumbled.

"Thanks. It was Samuel's idea. He likes the way I look without glasses."

Of course, Dad had never suggested that *I* get contacts.

"I know Samuel seems like an ogre sometimes, but he can be very flattering and sweet when he wants to be."

Hearing Jackie talk about Dad like that made me want to gag. I was mad enough that Dad allowed her to cook dinner that night. Then he had the audacity to volunteer *my* kitchen. Only two women had cooked in that kitchen before Saturday night, and neither one of those women had been named Jackie.

Dad marched into the room wearing a polo shirt that

looked a little too tight across his chest. As he passed by me, he reached out and squeezed my shoulder.

Dad stuck his nose into one of the pots. "What's for dinner?"

"Steak and potatoes," Jackie replied.

He kissed her on the cheek. "My favorite."

I liked to think of myself as logical and levelheaded, but even the most rational daughter in the world wouldn't be able to deal with Jackie. She was not only replacing my mother, she was replacing *me*. She replaced me at basketball games, she prepared the meals that were mine to cook, she even got the affection that was meant for me.

Just before I was about to explode, the doorbell rang. It had to be David.

Dad walked to the living room with me trailing closely behind. He opened the door, and sure enough, my fairytale prince stood at the doorsteps. David looked very respectable in his khaki pants and navy blue, long-sleeved shirt. Sarah must have helped him with his clothes.

"Good evening, Mr. Lee," David said.

For a second, I thought Dad was going to slam the door shut. He looked at David long and hard, not saying anything, and slowly moved out of the way.

I took David's jacket. "Hey," I said. I furrowed my eyes at him. *Are you okay? I'm sorry Dad is acting like such an asshole.*

"Hey," he replied. He winked at me. *I'm fine*, his smile said. *I've met worse fathers.*

"It's nice to finally meet you, David," Jackie said as she entered the living room. She extended her hand to him. "I'm Jackie."

David gently shook her hand. "The food smells great."

"Thanks. You're just in time, it's almost ready." Jackie placed her hand on Dad's arm. "We're really glad to have you here. Aren't we, Samuel."

"Yes, of course," Dad said to David, with a smile stamped across his face. "Rhonda has told me some great things about you."

I have?

"Have you thought about going to USC or Clemson?" Dad continued. "Are you going to try out for the basketball team?"

David shook his head. "No, I'm not that good. Christopher McCullough is the only guy on our team skilled enough to play for a Division I school."

Dad's smile disappeared. He probably wanted to pound his fist through the wall (or worse, through David's chest). I knew Dad's heart was beating at one hundred miles an hour, because *my* heart was beating at one hundred miles an hour. I hated how Christopher still had that power over us.

"I plan on going to Francis Marion University. They offered me a partial scholarship to play basketball, and I…"

David let his words drift off. He must have realized Dad was no longer paying attention to him.

I grabbed David's arm. "Let me show you to the bathroom, so you can wash up for dinner."

David nodded quickly, and he and I escaped from the living room.

"I'm sorry," David asked as soon as we were in the bathroom. "I shouldn't have brought up Christopher."

"Don't worry about it." I faked a smile. "Dad's always grumpy before he eats."

"Is there anything I should do?" he continued as he washed his hands. "Should I apologize or something?"

"I think you should just drop it."

"But I really wanted to make a good first impression." He shook his hands, spraying water across the mirror and walls.

"You know, we do have towels," I snapped.

David stopped shaking his hands. "Are you mad at me, too?"

"I'm…just drop it, okay?"

David didn't say anything else. He just dried his hands off on the towel and left for the dining room.

I cupped my hands under the faucet and splashed my face with water. After patting my face dry, I practiced grinning a few times in the mirror.

By the time I entered the dining room everyone else was seated. I slipped into the chair beside David, and quietly reached under the table and squeezed his knee. The corners of David's lips curved upward just a little. He reached over and squeezed my hand. And just like that, we were okay again.

Dad said a quick prayer, and we began passing around the food. It took everything in my power not to throw a huge heap of mashed potatoes on my plate. I glanced at Dad's plate. He had enough food stacked in front of him to feed two people.

We all focused on our plates and chewed our food in silence. I wasn't sure what I was supposed to say. I had never shared a meal with David or Jackie before. When Dad and I ate dinner, we usually talked about school, work, the weather—you know, the safe subjects. It wasn't in our programming to have a real conversation.

Dad finally cleared his throat. "So David, I hear your sister is pregnant."

What the fuck? Dad couldn't talk to me about my pregnancy, but he could bring up Sarah's *in the middle of dinner?*

David nodded. "She's almost twenty weeks along."

"I didn't realize she was so far along," Jackie mumbled. She quickly picked up her glass of wine and took a long sip. Over the rim of her glass, she glared at my father.

"She hasn't gained much weight yet," I said. "She's hardly showing."

Dad cut a slice of steak. "Lucky her."

The room became quiet for a few agonizing seconds. Jackie tilted her head back and downed her glass of wine.

She smiled weakly at us. "I think I'm going to need a refill."

 ∴

"Well, that was a complete disaster," I said after David and I walked outside of the house. We had forced ourselves through thirty minutes of torture by silence, laced with snippets of conversation. At least the food was edible.

"Dinner wasn't that bad," David said. "Your dad seems nice."

I rolled my eyes.

"Well, Jackie seems nice."

"I hate her," I said. "And you're supposed to hate her too, remember?"

"Sorry, I'll try to hate her come tomorrow." David took my hand and intertwined his fingers with mine. It was amazing how something as simple as holding hands could make me feel so warm and secure.

"You look really nice tonight," David whispered. He started to lean into me, and I immediately pulled away from him.

"For all I know, Dad could be watching us right now."

"I just wanted an innocent kiss."

I laughed sarcastically. "There isn't such a thing as an innocent kiss." I was supposed to sound witty, but I came off as bitter instead.

David frowned. "You've been acting strange all night. What's wrong?"

"Why does something have to be wrong with me?"

David stepped back and deeply exhaled. He didn't speak—he just stared at me with a gaze that made me want to curl up beside him and have him wrap his arms around me.

"Tell me something about yourself," he finally said.

"Why?" I demanded. I didn't mean to sound defensive, but it was a force of habit. I had been a loner for so long, it was difficult opening up to someone—I didn't even know if I *wanted* to open up to someone.

"I just want to know you better," he said.

"Well, what about you?" I asked. "Why don't we talk about you?"

"What do you want to know? My favorite basketball team? My favorite food?"

"Duke and pizza," I said.

"Okay, ask me something harder."

I thought for a second, and then said, way too quickly, "Why do you dislike your father so much?"

David paused and chewed on his bottom lip. Finally he shrugged. "He left."

"You mean he and your mother got divorced."

"My parents only got divorced four years ago. My father hasn't lived with us since I was eight."

"What happened?"

"He had another family," David said. "He decided to play daddy to the two kids he had with his secretary."

I moved closer to David. "I'm sorry."

"Don't be," he said. "Dad was a bully. We're better off without him."

Immediately, thoughts of Christopher and his father came to mind. "Did he…hit you?"

He shook his head, and I sighed in relief. "My father may be a jerk, but he isn't stupid."

"Maybe it's a rule that all fathers are jerks."

"Your father is strict because he cares about you. My father is mean because he enjoys pushing people around," he said. "Believe me, there's a big difference."

David's smile almost had me believing that my father wasn't as bad as I knew he was. Then David stepped toward me, and I forgot all about my father. "So now what?" he asked. "You want to talk some more?"

I shook my head. He smiled and slid my glasses off my nose. The house turned into a fuzzy haze, but David's face stayed crisp and clear. (Thank God I'm not far-sighted.)

His lips floated inches from my lips. "I don't know if I've actually said this before, but I really, really like you."

I nodded.

"And you like me, right?"

Again, I nodded.

"So if it's okay with you, I'd like to kiss you now, before I lose my nerve."

Before I could say *okay*, *please do*, *fine by me*, or anything else, he was kissing me. His lips were soft and warm, like I had always imagined them.

And then, before I lost *my* nerve, I kissed him back.

chapter[19]
the butterfly(effect)

"I can't believe you don't want to know what the sex of the baby is," I said as I drove Sarah from the doctor's office. School was out today because of a teacher workday, so I got the great fortune of shuttling Sarah to her doctor's appointment. "You have to be curious."

"Of course I'm curious," she said. "But it doesn't matter—I've already picked out names for the baby. I'll name him David if he's a boy and Rhonda if she's a girl."

I laughed. "Come on, you can come up with something better than that. I wouldn't wish my name on anyone. And David is such a common name."

Sarah flipped down the overhead mirror and started finger-combing her hair. "It's a biblical name."

"And when's the last time you went to church?" Sarah's idea of church was watching hip-hop gospel videos on cable.

"I've actually been going to church more."

I almost drove off the road. "What? Since when did you become religious?"

Sarah stopped teasing her hair. "A woman in my Childbirth Education class invited me to church. I went, and I actually liked it." She wrapped her hands around her stomach. "I don't know what it is, but when I'm sitting inside that sanctuary, listening to a beautiful choir, I feel…"

"Safe?"

Sarah nodded. "Yeah. Safe."

"Well, I still think you should come up with some better boy names. How about Richard or Bradley." At this point, my mouth was working faster than my brain. "Maybe you could name the baby after his…"

Sarah frowned. "Maybe I could name the baby after his *what*?"

I gulped. "Maybe you could name the baby after his father."

Sarah didn't say anything for the rest of the drive back to her house. Up until now, I had done a pretty good job of avoiding the topic of her baby's father. Even when David hounded me for information, I didn't talk about the father. Of course, the only reason I didn't talk about the father was because I didn't know who he was. Sarah wasn't able to keep her pregnancy a secret, but her sperm donor's identity was anyone's guess.

I pulled into her driveway and parked next to David's car. "Does the father know you're pregnant?" I felt myself cringing as I asked the question.

Sarah nodded.

"How did he take the news?"

She rubbed at the two silver bracelets on her wrist. "The only way he could—he proposed."

"What?"

"Don't worry," she said. "I don't have any intention of getting married."

I waited for Sarah to continue, but she seemed content with the information she had given. I decided to press the issue.

"Is he someone I know?"

"Rhonda…"

Bad idea.

"I'm sorry," I said. "I know I promised that I wouldn't ask you questions about him."

"Then don't," she said. "I'll eventually tell you who he is, after he's had some time to deal with my pregnancy. I've had a lot longer than he has to come to terms with it."

I stepped out of the car. It took Sarah twice as long as it took me to climb out of my bucket seats. She was only twenty-four weeks pregnant, but she was already having trouble with daily activities. She hadn't worn a pair of lace-up shoes for at least a month.

We entered the house, and Sarah flung her keys on the table. She picked up a slip of paper and crinkled her nose as she read the message.

"A note from your mother?" I asked.

Sarah nodded. She and her mother were at odds again, using David as the go-between. When he wasn't available, good old-fashioned pen and paper had to do the trick.

"Gail called," Sarah said. "Did you tell her you were coming over here?"

I nodded. "David and I are supposed to catch a movie with her, Xavier, and Xavier's girlfriend." I glanced at Sarah out of the corner of my eye as I picked up the phone. "You're welcome to come along if you want to."

Sarah laughed. "The last thing I want to do is wedge my butt into some movie theater seat," she said. "But thanks for asking."

I dialed Gail's number, and she picked up on the first ring. "We've got a situation," she said. "Xavier's drunk."

"What? Since when did he start drinking?"

"Michelle broke up with him this afternoon, and I guess he decided to drown his sorrows in Colt 45," she said. "I can't send him back home in this state, and my folks are liable to walk in any second now. Can we stay over at your place until Xavier sobers up?"

"No way. Dad's at home tonight." I glanced at Sarah, as she leaned against the wall, her hands on her belly.

"Is everything okay?" Sarah asked.

I put my hand over the receiver. "Xavier's drunk. Can we bring him over here?"

Sarah nodded. "Sure. Mom's at a conference in Boston this weekend."

I brought the receiver back to my mouth. "Bring him over to Sarah's house."

There was a long pause on the other end of the phone. "Gail…"

"I'm thinking," she replied.

I shook my head. "It's not like we have much of a choice."

She sighed. "Okay. I'll be there in a few minutes."

I hung up the phone and turned to Sarah. "Why don't you brew a pot of coffee? I need to talk to David."

Sarah nodded, and as she headed to the pantry, I turned down the hallway and made my way to David's room. I stood outside of his door for what seemed like hours. I had passed by his room countless times on the way to Sarah's room, but I had never entered it.

I finally knocked on the door.

"Come in."

I opened the door. David stood at his dresser with his shirt off. I didn't have a true appreciation of David's physique until that moment. His stomach was flat, and his shoulders and arms were extremely well defined.

David and I had been going out for almost a month, but our physical relationship hadn't advanced much further than a few passionate kisses. He did a very good job of keeping his hands in all the correct places and I tried to do the same. As I looked at his chest, I realized I was missing out on quite a treat.

"Hey," David said. He seemed a little taken aback to see me standing at his door. "I didn't know you were here."

"We just got back."

He reached into a drawer and pulled out a black T-shirt. He didn't look to be in any hurry to put it on, and truthfully, I wasn't in any hurry to have him put it on.

"I don't think we're gonna make it to the movies tonight," I said.

"Why?" David walked over to me, his torso still exposed. "Is something wrong?"

I forced myself to look at his face instead of his chest. "Michelle broke up with Xavier, and he's taking it pretty bad." I leaned closer to him. He smelled like he had just stepped out of the shower. "He's also a little drunk," I whispered. "Gail's on her way over here now with him."

"I see. You have to play the responsible friend tonight." He smiled, and for a second I forgot about Xavier and Gail and everyone else in the world. "It's okay. We'll go out another time."

"Are you sure? You could still go to the movie—"

"It's okay," he said, finally putting on his shirt. "Anyway, I wasn't going to watch the movie. I was going to watch you." He leaned over and planted a kiss on my earlobe.

I felt my face getting hot. Ever since we had started

seeing each other, I felt less and less depressed about not getting the scholarship to Georgia Tech. I had even reduced my weekly ice cream intake to a half-scoop. David's sugary-sweet kisses more than made up for all the calories I was missing out on.

Grudgingly, I backed away from David. "We'd better head to the kitchen. Gail and Xavier will be here pretty soon."

David and I went back to the kitchen and started piling snacks on the table while Sarah scooped coffee grounds into the coffee machine. Just as the coffee had finished brewing, the doorbell rang.

"I'll get it," I said, already heading toward the living room.

I opened the door. Gail stood at the doorway, her arms folded tight across her chest. Xavier slouched behind her. His eyes were red and droopy.

"How much has he had to drink?" I asked.

Gail shrugged. "At least two forty-ounces. Probably more."

Xavier puffed out his chest. "I'm not drunk. I'm liberated."

She shook her head. "He's been like this ever since he showed up at my house."

"Come on," I said. "Sarah's pouring him a cup of coffee now."

Gail marched toward the kitchen, her arms still folded across her chest. Xavier zigzagged behind her.

Xavier staggered into the kitchen, took one look at Sarah, and smiled. "Hey, Sarah," he gushed. "You know, you're really pretty. Much prettier than *her*."

"Good Lord," Gail said. "Someone please shoot me now."

I took Xavier by the arm and led him to the table. "What happened?"

"She dumped me. For another guy."

I wanted to explain that it was probably better for her to dump him for another guy than a girl, but I figured that point might be lost on Xavier at the current moment.

"She said I wasn't edgy enough. She thought I was a real writer. Like Hemingway." Xavier smiled. "Hemingway drank a lot. I figured I'd do the same thing."

"Hemingway also shot himself in the head with a shotgun," I said. "You gonna do that too?"

Xavier scratched his chin. "Well, drinking seemed like a good idea at the time."

"Try this," Sarah said as she placed a steaming mug of coffee on the table. "It'll make you feel better."

As Xavier hung his head over his coffee, Sarah, Gail, David, and I huddled together in the living room. Gail narrowed her eyes at me. "I'm not gonna say I told you so, but—"

"Gail, please. You'll have plenty of time to gloat later about how right you were and how wrong everyone else was." I turned to David. "Maybe you should talk to him."

"But I don't know what to say," he whispered back.

"Haven't you ever consoled a guy when he got dumped?"

"Of course not. Real guys don't get all teary-eyed over some girl dropping them. They just move on to the next girl."

Sarah, Gail, and I crossed our arms and stared at David.

He shrugged. "What? It's the truth."

"Will you just go and say something to him?" I said. "Before I drop *you*."

We all headed back to the kitchen. Xavier's face was immersed in steam from the coffee. "Hey man, sorry to hear about the girlfriend." David patted Xavier on the shoulder. "But you're probably better off without her."

Xavier replied, but his words were too slurred for me to understand.

"You should probably do something to get her off your mind," he said. "You want to go play basketball or something?"

"The last time I played basketball, I broke my ankle."

David frowned and looked up at us. Gail and I nodded. "Last summer," I said.

He turned back to Xavier. "Well, do you play video games? I've got the lastest—"

"I'm not really that good with video games." He took a quick sip of coffee. "My parents thought my time would be better spent reading."

David sighed. "Well, what do you want to do?"

Xavier looked up. "I wanna get laid."

David removed his hand from Xavier's shoulder.

"Sorry, but I can't help you out with that one." He shuffled back to us. "That's all I got. You're on your own." He leaned over to peck me on the cheek. "Maybe I should go to Johnnie's house."

"Can I go with you?" Gail asked.

"None of you are going anywhere," I said. "Xavier's really depressed right now. We need to help him."

Gail shook her head. "I can't deal with all of this whining. It isn't logical."

"Of course it isn't logical," Sarah said. "He was in love."

Gail huffed. "Not this love crap again."

Sarah crossed her arms. "I'm sorry Gail, but it *is* possible for a high school student to fall in love." She nodded toward Xavier. "Let me try to talk to him."

Sarah walked to the table and sat beside Xavier. He immediately smiled again. "Xavier, you shouldn't be so hard on yourself. You're too good to be dating a girl like Michelle."

"But—"

"How many times did you take her out?" Sarah asked.

"I don't know." He drank more of his coffee. "Maybe six times over the past few months."

"Did she ever offer to pay when y'all went to the movies?"

He shook his head.

"What about when y'all went to dinner? Did she pay then?"

Again, he shook his head.

"I'm no economist, but the way it sounds, you spent a lot of money," she said. "And it sounds like you didn't get a good return on your investment."

"I did spend a lot of money on her. I even bought us tickets to our prom." He sat up a little. "I guess you wouldn't be interested in going to the prom, would you?"

"Thanks for the offer, sweetie, but I don't think they sell prom dresses in the maternity section of Macy's." Sarah looked at Gail. "But I'm sure Gail will go with you."

Gail started toward the table, her hands balled into fists. "I most certainly will not—"

"It's not like her boyfriend would be around to go with her anyway," Sarah continued. "And Gail is a good friend."

Xavier beamed at Gail. "She's a great friend," he said. "She only cursed at me once on the way over here."

Gail sighed and loosened her hands. "Okay, I'll go with you, but we are *not* wearing matching colors."

David laughed and wrapped his arms around me. "So now what?"

I leaned into my boyfriend. I didn't know which was better—the sound of his voice or the feel of his hands on me. "We hang out and watch a few movies while we wait for Xavier to throw up," I replied.

Xavier staggered to his feet. "Really, guys, I don't feel that bad." Then a hiccup exploded from his mouth, and he slouched back down into his seat. "Rhonda, why didn't you ever tell me drinking felt so good?"

I headed to the counter to pour Xavier another cup of coffee. "I promise you, it doesn't feel nearly as good when you're kneeling face first in front of a toilet."

David ventured closer to Xavier. "Do you still feel tipsy?"

"Of course he does," Gail answered. "Xavier gets tipsy from drinking cough syrup."

I placed a fresh cup of coffee in front of him. "Is the coffee helping?"

"I don't think so. If anything, I'm still as drunk, but now I'm hyper as well." He motioned for me to move closer to him. "And I have to pee," he whispered before erupting into a fit of laughter. Then suddenly, he jumped up and put his hand to his mouth.

"I think I'm gonna be sick," he said before running off down the hallway.

I just shook my head. Maybe it wasn't too late for *all* of us to go to Johnnie's house.

∴

Sure enough, Xavier spent most of the night throwing up. While he spent the rest of the night curled into a ball on the bathroom floor, the rest of us played cards and watched movies. And while I wasn't 100 percent sure, I think I noticed Gail smiling during the evening, if only for a few seconds.

After Xavier finally emerged from the bathroom, we

poured a bottle of mouthwash down his throat and got him ready to take home. I walked Gail and Xavier to her car while David and Sarah figured out how to best sanitize their bathroom.

"Thanks for everything," Gail said after we pushed Xavier into the car. "I don't know what I would have done with Xavier without you."

"Don't forget Sarah."

Gail paused. "Yeah, I guess she isn't that bad."

Did Gail just compliment Sarah? Maybe she was the one who was drunk.

"Don't look at me like that," Gail said. "She did get Xavier to stop whining, even though now I've got to go to prom with him."

Xavier stretched out across Gail's back seat and placed his hands over his ears. "Why are you guys yelling?" he moaned.

Gail slammed her door shut, which made Xavier writhe in even more agony. "That's what you get for getting drunk."

I shook my head. Gail was as firm a believer in tough-love as I had ever seen. "Well, I'd better get out of here," I said as I lifted my sleeve to look at my watch. "I don't want to miss my—*Shit!*"

"What?"

I yanked my keys out of my pocket. "It's ten minutes to midnight."

"So?"

"Some of us have a curfew, remember? I'm gonna be late."

Her eyes widened. "*Oh.* You're screwed," she said. "Maybe it'll help if you tell your father about Xavier getting drunk."

"You're kidding, right? Knowing him, that'll just make things worse." I jogged toward my car. "Do me a favor and tell David why I had to leave."

She nodded, and I jumped into my car. Two seconds later, I was peeling out of the driveway.

I watched as my speedometer jumped to twenty miles over the speed limit. I was only going to be a few minutes late. Maybe he wouldn't be awake. Maybe my watch was running fast.

I zoomed past a stop sign. Maybe he was with Jackie. Maybe he was out on another of his all-night dates.

I pulled into the driveway and leapt out of the car. As I dashed toward the house, I glanced at my watch again. Only ten minutes late. Surely, even *he* couldn't get mad for something like that.

I swung open the door, and there Dad stood. He looked down at his watch, and then glared at me. "You're late."

I meekly smiled at him. "Only by a few minutes."

Dad didn't smile back. "Rhonda, how am I supposed to trust you when you can't even follow simple directions? It's things like this that remind me why I'm glad you didn't get that scholarship from Georgia Tech. Obviously, you're not responsible enough to live away from home just yet."

Leave it to Dad to find a way to put an exclamation point on an already crappy evening.

I sighed. "I'm sorry I was late."

"Sorry just isn't good enough," he snapped. "You're grounded."

I knew there was no point in arguing with him. He was right. He was always right.

"For how long?"

He rubbed his chin for a few moments. "One month," he finally said.

My mouth dropped open. "You can't be serious! This is the first time I've broken curfew in years." I shook my head. "Talk about unfair. You get to stay out all night with Jackie, and I'm getting grounded for being ten minutes late!"

"I'm an adult. You're not." He crossed his arms and peered down at me. "Where did you go tonight?"

"I spent the entire night at Sarah's house. We were just watching TV and playing cards."

"Was her mother there?"

"No," I mumbled.

His eyes widened. "You were there alone with that boy?"

"Of course not. Sarah, Gail, and Xavier were there as well."

Dad didn't say anything for a few moments. He popped his knuckles a few times, all the while keeping his gaze glued to the ground.

"You're having sex again, aren't you?"

"What? Of course not!"

Even though I was screaming like a lunatic, Dad was able to keep his voice low and steady. "Rhonda, don't lie to me."

"I'm not lying!"

My father could be such an asshole sometimes. It wasn't the words that Dad said, it was the way he said them. Like it was already a matter of fact. He wasn't asking—he was telling me what he already knew. He was always right, even when he was wrong.

Dad shook his head. "You know what, I don't even want to know what happened between you and that boy."

I felt like I was going to explode. "His name is David!"

Dad shrugged. "I don't care what his name is. All I know is, come Monday morning, we're putting you on birth control."

"Dad!"

"I don't want to hear it, Rhonda. I can't stop you from having sex, but I'll be damned if you get pregnant again."

I wagged my finger at him. "Dad, you can't control me like that. You have no right to say what I am and what I'm not going to do."

"I'm your father. I can do anything I damn well please to protect my child."

"I'm not a child anymore."

"You said the same thing three years ago. Look where that got you."

I slammed my hand on the table. "God, I hate you!"

It was an immature thing to say, but I couldn't think of anything else to yell at him.

Dad looked like he didn't care whether I loved him or hated him at that point. "I'm sorry, but this isn't up for discussion."

I pushed past him as my eyes started to water. "Wait here. I need to show you something."

I stormed into my room, yanked open my top dresser drawer, and grabbed my package of birth control pills. They had been in the same place, under my pajamas, that I had hid them since my freshman year.

I ran back to the kitchen and flung the package of pills at Dad. I aimed for his face. Unfortunately, it bounced off his chest and fell to the floor.

"As you can see, there's nothing to discuss," I said, my voice breaking. "You don't have to put me on the pill, because I'm already on it."

Dad knelt down to pick up the package. "How long…?"

"Three years," I said. "Ever since the abortion, I've been too afraid to have sex, but I'm still on the goddamn pill."

"Why didn't you tell me?"

"Because it was none of your business."

"Yes, it is—"

"No, it isn't," I said. "You no longer have any say over what I do with my body. That ended on the day you made me get that abortion."

"We *both* decided that it was best for you to have the procedure."

"That's bullshit and you know it." I marched to him and poked my finger into his chest. "You forced me to get that abortion."

Dad's eyes finally softened. "I had no idea you felt this way."

I continued to poke him. "And what if David and I *did* have sex? What if we *were* sleeping together? At least he's not afraid to touch me." I grabbed Dad's hand. "Why don't you hug me anymore?"

"I hug you—"

"No, you don't," I said. "Ever since the abortion, you've treated me like shit. Why don't we go to basketball games anymore? Why don't we watch the Braves on television?" I released his hand, and he cradled it like it had been burned. "I'm not good enough for you anymore, but Jackie is?"

Dad took a step back. "I'm...I'm sorry."

My entire body began to tremble. "*Now* you want to apologize?"

"I'm so sorry, Rhonda. I didn't know..."

"You think just because you apologize that everything is going to be okay?" I stepped toward him and planted my hands on my hips. "You can't just say a few words and erase the past three years."

Dad slowly placed his hands on my shoulders. "Rhonda, you have to understand. If I had known how you felt, I would have acted differently. Maybe if I had been around more, or maybe if I had been a better father…"

I brushed his hands off me. "I can't believe you're making this about you. I'm the one that had the abortion, remember?"

Dad opened his arms and inched toward me. "Honey, I'm sorry. I only did what I thought was best." He began to wrap his arms around me, my pills still firmly in his grasp. "Can you forgive me?"

"Like I said before, it's a little late for apologies." I stepped out of Dad's embrace and snatched the birth control pills from his hand. "Now if you'll excuse me, I have a pill to take."

As I spun on my heels and marched to my room, I mentally added a new rule to my life:

Postulate 5:
My father will never make another decision for me.
Ever.

chapter[20]
combining like(terms)

Helen and I walked into the department store and made a beeline for the formalwear section. This was the third store we had been to, and we still hadn't found a suitable dress.

"Are you sure you want to buy me a dress?" I asked. "Some of them are pretty expensive."

"Like I said before, it's my treat," she replied. "Think of it as a reward for getting a scholarship to Georgia Tech."

I had received the letter earlier that week informing me of the partial scholarship I was awarded. While it wasn't a full ride, it would cover the majority of my tuition. The way I calculated it, if I worked twenty hours a week while in school, I would have enough money to cover all of my expenses, without my father's help.

Dad was so ecstatic when he found out about the scholarship, he lifted my one-month punishment (never mind the fact that I had no intention of abiding by it). He even took the letter to his office and showed it to all of his co-workers. For once, it seemed like I did something right in my father's eyes.

Ever since the night of our argument, Dad and I had been walking on eggshells when we were around each other. Dad wasn't offering to help me get ready for the prom, and I wasn't asking. As long as I stayed out of his way and he stayed out of mine, I figured we could survive in our social stalemate for the rest of the school year.

"I can't believe your prom is in two weeks," Helen said, bringing me back to the task at hand. She started looking through the leftover dresses on one of the bargain racks. "Why did you wait so long to buy a dress?"

"I wanted to lose some weight."

"We could have gotten the dress taken in if you lost weight," she said. "How many pounds did you lose?"

"Seven."

Well, it would have been seven, if pounds were counted like dog years.

"How is Samuel acting about all of this?" Helen asked. "It's got to be a big deal for his baby girl to be going to her first prom."

"I'm not his baby girl anymore."

Helen sighed. "You know what I mean."

I walked to another rack and picked up a sequined lime-green dress. "He's treating the prom like he treats everything else. He's ignoring the topic entirely. I just hope he doesn't change his mind at the last minute and decide that I can't go."

"He'll let you go," she said. "You know, your father and mother met at a dance in college."

"Really?" I momentarily forgot about the hideous dress in my hands. "He never told me that."

She smiled. "You should ask him about some of the old times."

I shook my head. "Dad and I don't talk much anymore."

Helen stopped flipping through dresses and walked over to me. "Rhonda, isn't it time you forgave him?"

I quickly looked around the store. Groups of mothers and teenage girls were scattered throughout the formal-wear department. "I don't want to have this conversation now." I turned my attention back to the dress rack.

"If not now, then when?" Helen placed her hands on my shoulders and forced me to look at her. Her child-like freckles stood in contrast to the wisdom she usually gave. "In a few months, you'll be in college. Do you really want to leave things like they are between you and your father?"

"I love Dad. He's a great provider and a good family

man," I said, before shaking my head. "But I can't forgive him for making me end my pregnancy."

"Don't you think you were too young—"

"I don't know!" I looked around as a few mother-daughter combos glanced in our direction. I stepped closer to her. "But I should have had the opportunity to make that decision," I whispered.

"You were running out of time."

"It was still my choice."

Helen sighed, and her green eyes washed over me like a rising tide. "Well, if you can't forgive him, can you at least forgive yourself?"

"Forgive myself?" I shook her hands off me and continued looking through the dresses. "I didn't do anything wrong."

I didn't do anything but have sex, get pregnant, and have an abortion.

Helen moved to the other side of the circular rack. "Has David picked out his tux yet?"

I felt myself smiling at the mention of his name. "I think so. He's been hounding me for weeks about what color I was wearing."

"Have y'all made any plans for after the prom?"

"No. We'll probably just go back to his house and hang out with Sarah."

Helen reemerged on my side of the rack with three dresses. I immediately frowned at the first one she showed me. Too much lace.

"Prom's a very *special* night for some teenagers."

What was going on with Helen? All of a sudden, she was a walking after-school special.

"Come on, Helen. You know I'm not a virgin, and he isn't either." I held up the second dress to my body. It was wide enough, but was made for someone five inches taller than me.

"Just because you two have already done the deed doesn't mean that prom still isn't a special night." She scrunched up her nose at the remaining dress in her hand and went to the back side of the rack to return the dresses. "So are y'all sleeping together?" she asked, as casually as if she was asking the time of day. "I know you really like him."

I stormed around the rack and planted myself in front of Helen. "What's with all the questions?" I asked. "You're starting to sound like Dad."

"I'm sorry. I'm not trying to pry. It's just that someone has to ask these questions, and I know you aren't talking to your father." She paused and fingered my hair. "It's what your mother would want me to do."

Just because it was something my mother would approve of didn't automatically get Helen off the hook. "Yes, I like him a lot. But we're going to two different colleges. We probably won't even be together by August."

"A lot can happen between now and August."

I took a deep breath. "I haven't had sex with him, and I don't plan on having sex with him."

Helen beamed at me. "Good answer." She pulled out

one more dress. "But just in case you change your mind, be sure to use a condom."

"Helen!"

She laughed. "Your mother would be so proud of you."

．．

Helen and I didn't find any dresses that Wednesday. Or that Thursday. On Saturday morning, we hit the last of the stores in Columbia. Still nothing. I was beginning to think that maybe I had passed on that lime-green sequined dress too soon.

David and I had a much-needed date on Saturday night. Between school, tutoring, the search for prom dresses, and drunk friends, we had barely seen each other. And like most of our other dates, this one ended much too soon.

"What did you think of the movie?" I asked, as David parked outside of his house. I had driven over there earlier, but we took David's car to the movie. After the failed dinner attempt, I felt it would be easier on all parties for me to meet David at his house rather than have him and Dad come face to face.

David shrugged. "It was very…entertaining."

"So you didn't mind going to a chick flick with me?"

"Of course I didn't mind," he said. "Why would I want to see a movie filled with mind-numbing violence, gratuitous sex, and loads of profanity? I'd much rather spend two hours watching melodramatic, tear-inducing reunions and heartfelt confessions of undying love."

I grinned and wrapped my arm in his. "That's why you're so great. But to be fair, I told you I didn't mind watching it with Sarah and Gail."

"There was no way I was letting you cancel on me like you did a couple of weeks ago." He snuggled next to me. "The way I see it, you owe me, big time."

"Oh, really?" I crossed my arms. "And just what do you have in mind?"

David looked up at his big, empty house. "Well, I *do* have the house all to myself. And you know I'm afraid of the dark…"

There we were, flirting again. And there I was, enjoying it.

"When is everyone getting back into town?" I asked.

"Sarah will be back tomorrow morning. Mom will be back on Monday. Or Thursday. Or the following week."

Sarah had decided to spend the weekend in Charleston with her father. Ms. Gamble was…well, we weren't quite sure where she was.

"Enough talk about my family." David ran his palm against the side of my face, slightly grazing the tip of my earlobe. A warm feeling flashed through me. Then he kissed me, and the warm feeling turned boiling hot.

After a few passionate kisses, David pulled away from me. "I'd better let you go. If you're not home by midnight, your father will have a fit."

"He would have a fit, *if* he were home. He and Jackie went to some type of formal banquet tonight, so he won't be home until late. That is, if he comes home at all tonight."

"He and Jackie seem to be getting pretty close."

I frowned. "Don't remind me."

"Well, if you don't have to go, you can come in for a few minutes…"

David was kidding again, of course. For some reason, I decided not to joke back.

"Sure, I'll stay for a while."

"Yeah, right." He pecked me on the nose. "You'd better get home."

I stuffed my keys back into my pocket and headed for the front door. "David, I'm serious. I can come in for a few minutes."

"Are you sure?" He looked around, like he expected someone to jump from the bushes at any second. "It's kinda late."

I rolled my eyes. "I'm not asking to spend the night. I just want to hang out with you for a little longer." I glanced at my watch. "I have almost an hour before my curfew."

"Um, okay." David opened the door and let me enter first. I wasn't sure how he felt about all of this. Most guys would love to get a girl alone in their house. However, as David had pointed out before, he wasn't like most guys.

There was just enough moonlight filtering through

the windows so that I could maneuver around the room. I took my jacket off and flung it across the sofa before sitting down and picking up the remote. Nothing was on but the usual trash on cable. I flipped through channels until I found the sports network.

"Is basketball okay?" I asked. "The game looks pretty good."

"It's better than the crap we watched at the movie theater."

I would have argued with him, but he was right. I'd take a good basketball game over a movie full of whiny females any day.

David sat on the opposite end of the couch from me. Over the span of three time-outs, he slowly inched his way over to me. It was almost cute.

"This is a pretty good game," he said.

"Yeah, it's very exciting."

"Yeah…exciting."

We sat there for a few seconds, submerged in silence. But if you listened very closely, you could hear the faint hum of nervous energy bouncing all around us. My entire being was filled with anxious anticipation. But what was I anticipating?

"Well, I guess I'd better go," I said.

"Yeah, I guess so."

Neither of us moved.

"You want to watch the rest of the game?" I asked.

"No, you can turn the TV off."

I turned off the television. Immediately, the room went pitch black. Two human statues sat on the couch, surrounded by an eerie darkness.

"I didn't realize it was so dark out—"

Before I could finish my sentence, David's body was pressed against me, his mouth moving furiously against mine.

David paused from kissing long enough to remove my glasses from my face and place them on the coffee table. Then the distance between his face and mine disappeared, and we were kissing again. I wrapped my arms around him and kissed him faster, harder, stronger than I ever had before.

Somehow, we ended up horizontal on the couch, him on top of me, our legs twisted together. Minutes passed like seconds. I felt ravenous.

I had always thought that David was a good kisser, but he was easily surpassing his previous best performance. He alternated between holding my hands and running his fingers through my hair. Only once did David's hand grace the side of my body, and even then he didn't venture to any of the forbidden zones. I knew he wanted to. He *had* to have wanted to. But I also knew he wouldn't go there unless I let him know it was okay.

Was it okay?

I answered my own question by taking his hand in mine and slowly guiding it to my chest. As impossible as I thought it was, our kisses became more passionate. My heart thundered. I was restless and scared and excited all at once. This may have been David's first visit to the land of Rhonda, but he navigated all my peaks and valleys like a seasoned explorer.

I began pulling at his shirt because I wanted to run my hands over his back. Maybe he thought I was trying to take his shirt completely off (and maybe I really was). But the next thing I knew, his shirt was off and flying across the room.

Seconds later, my arms were above my head, and he was slipping my blouse off. I didn't even try to stop him. In the middle of the day, I would have been self-conscious of my less-than-perfect body. But in the darkness of his house, I felt beautiful.

We stayed like this for a few moments. We could have set the couch on fire with the amount of heat we were generating. My mouth, my nose, my cheeks, my neck, my chest—his lips were going everywhere across my body. It was like I hoped it would be, only better.

David reached around my back and began pawing at my bra strap. His fingers brushed against those three hooks like he was strumming a guitar. After a few feeble attempts, he stopped and switched hands.

If I were cruel, I would have let him suffer all night (I had done it to Christopher on more than one occasion). But I liked him better than that. And to be honest, I really wanted that bra off.

I reached behind my back and unfastened my bra with

a flick of my fingers. I was topless, and I loved it. I didn't think a pair of hands could feel so good against my skin, but his felt wonderful. They weren't cold and prodding like Christopher's. His touch was soft and gentle.

We flipped and tussled some more. I didn't care about the time or the place. His hand slipped to my zipper, and I tensed up, if only for an instant. Slowly, he peeled the zipper down. Then his hand slipped into my jeans.

I gasped. I moaned. I floated outside of my body.

Then I felt David tugging at my jeans. A small alarm went off in my head. By the time they were pulled to mid-thigh, a siren was blaring full blast in my brain. I had lived this "fairy tale" before. The ending sucked for the princess.

"I think we should stop," I mumbled.

"What?" David asked, as he struggled for air. His bare chest pressed against mine like we were sharing the same skin. He nuzzled against my face and nibbled on my ear.

I pushed him away from me. "I said to stop."

David froze, his mouth hovering over my cheek. Then he jumped off me. David withdrew to the edge of the couch and stared straight ahead.

"I'm sorry," he said, talking faster than his lips could move. "I didn't hear what you said at first. I didn't—"

"It's okay." I tried to cover my chest with one arm, while I pulled up my jeans with my free hand. This scene was also very familiar, and very distasteful.

David kept his gaze off of me, allowing me *some* dignity as my hands fumbled through the darkness, searching for my missing clothes. I found my bra sandwiched between the cushions of the couch. My blouse was on the floor, balled up in a heap.

I wasn't sure which of us felt more ashamed. I knew David felt like he did something wrong, even though he didn't do anything I didn't allow him to do. But I, on the other hand, got so caught up in the moment that I almost threw away everything I had worked so hard for. I was a good girl now. I didn't do stuff like this anymore, even with guys I really liked. It was too dangerous.

While I finished getting dressed, David went across the room and retrieved his shirt. I got up and walked to him, but he still wasn't looking at me. I wanted to wrap my arms around him and convince him it was okay, but I didn't. Maybe because it really wasn't okay. We had almost crossed a line we weren't even supposed to be close to.

"Will I see you tomorrow?" he asked.

I shrugged. "I doubt it. I think Sarah and I are meeting at Gail's house to study."

By the way he slumped his shoulders, I knew he didn't hear the answer he was hoping for. But I couldn't see him tomorrow. Tomorrow was too soon.

David reached out and kissed me. I began to get that wonderfully warm feeling I usually got, but I suppressed it. I forced myself to feel cold. I willed my lips to turn to stone.

"I'm sorry," he whispered into my hair. "I hope you're not mad at me."

"It's okay," I whispered back. "I'm not angry with you."

It was true—I wasn't angry with my boyfriend. I was angry with myself.

chapter[21]
addition by(subtraction)

I got home five minutes before curfew. Like I expected, Dad wasn't home. He didn't even call. When two o'clock came and went, I knew he wasn't coming home that night. Jackie had gotten her hooks into him, and he wouldn't resurface until early in the morning.

I tossed and turned in bed, my thick comforter shielding me from the chill of my room. I had ten pillows on my bed, but none of them felt comfortable underneath me. Every time I closed my eyes, I felt David's lips on my skin, his hands on my body. For a quick instant, I felt wonderful. Immediately afterwards, I was flooded with guilt and remorse.

Why did I let David touch me like that? Why did I have to like it so much? Things were much less complicated when we just held hands.

I had felt the same way after I first slept with Christopher. But at least then I could blame some of my stupidity on ignorance. I knew exactly what would happen at David's house, and I still put myself in that situation.

It was on a Saturday afternoon when I first slept with Christopher. It was a bright and sunny December day. For a few weeks, he had been promising to throw me a romantic picnic. Why he wanted to have a picnic in the wintertime, I didn't know. But he did, and like a fool, I bought into the idea.

The day was cool, but not cold. There wasn't a cloud in the sky. I felt like it was a perfect day for a perfect picnic with a perfect boyfriend.

Christopher picked me up in his mother's Saab. He had some old love songs playing on the stereo. He even opened the car door for me. We found a quiet, secluded corner of the park to set up his red-checkered picnic blanket, just like in the movies.

The day was going according to plan (well, according to *my* plan), until he brought out a bottle of red wine. It was fruity and sweet, and before I knew it we had emptied the bottle. And then, he said the magic words I was longing to hear.

I love you.

It was only a few minutes after he uttered those words that we were in the back seat of the car. We had gotten pretty hot and heavy before, but we hadn't gotten to the point where we were taking off clothes. At least, not until that day.

I was tipsy, but I wasn't drunk. I could have easily stopped him, but I didn't want to. *He loved me. And I loved him.* And I knew I would be with him forever.

Fast-forward a few months. We had broken up, and I was pregnant with his child.

As I agonized over how every little detail of my evening with David mimicked my first time, night transformed into morning. A new day was born right in front of my heavy, red, sleep-deprived eyes. Just like last time.

I finally forced myself to get out of bed and face my day. A huge stack of blueberry pancakes was calling my name, and I was in no position to argue with my appetite.

Just as I was pouring the homemade batter onto the griddle, I heard Dad's car pull into the yard. It was a little after six o'clock, and I knew he expected me to be asleep. He almost jumped out of his skin when he opened the door and saw me at the stove.

"Rhonda!" Dad yelled, clutching his chest. "What are you doing up this early in the morning?"

I shrugged. "I was hungry."

Dad had a guilty look on his face as he glanced at his watch. He was caught, red-handed. But he wasn't a teenage girl, so it must have been okay.

Dad trudged over to the stove, but of course he didn't come in physical contact with me. "Smells good," he said, sniffing the air.

I flipped over the pancake before stirring up the batter. "You want some?"

"No, I'm not hungry."

Dad, not hungry? The only time he didn't eat was when he was in a great mood. I glanced at the makeup stains on his jacket. He must have had a very good night.

Dad coughed a few times and rubbed the back of his neck. "How was your date?"

My hand froze in place, hovering over the bowl of batter. More than anything, I wanted to bolt out of that room, but my legs felt like they were cast in concrete. I was stuck. I was helpless.

"It went fine," I said.

"How was the movie?"

"Okay."

"I was thinking," he began, stepping toward me. "Maybe we could catch a movie this afternoon. Just me and you."

I kept my gaze glued to the stove. "I have plans."

"Then maybe next weekend?"

"Maybe."

Dad stared at me in silence for a few moments as I flipped a pancake. Finally, he sighed. "How long are we going to do this?"

A lump formed in my throat. I poked at the cooking pancake with my spatula, just to keep my hands busy. "Do what?"

"You know what I'm talking about," he said. "How

many times do I have to tell you I'm sorry before you for-give me?"

I didn't answer him, because I didn't know.

He continued to stand there, not saying anything. Then he stepped toward me and tried to wrap his arms around my shoulders. I pulled away.

Dad dropped his hands to his side. "I'll be in my room, if you need me."

I nodded, and Dad left the room. And there I was, alone with my food. Just like last time.

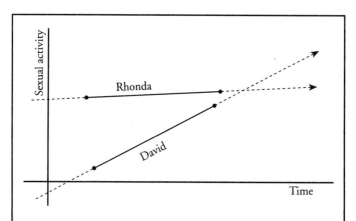

Geometry 101:

If two lines exist on the same plane, and if both lines have different slopes, they will eventually *intersect*.

However, line segments of said lines may not necessarily intersect, if the *end points* of each segment occur *before the point of intersection*.

By the time I emerged from my room on Monday morning, I knew what I had to do about David. As much as I hated to admit it, the postulates were never wrong. Guys like him weren't to be trusted. Rather, *I* wasn't to be trusted around guys like him. I was so close to graduation. I couldn't risk messing everything up for a silly high school romance.

I had to break up with him. It was the logical thing to do.

I decided to try to avoid David at school—it would be easier to break the news over the phone. When I got to school that morning, I headed straight to the library. During lunch, I camped out in my car and ate celery sticks. And after the final school bell rang, I spent an extra thirty minutes in class, just so I could wait him out. But apparently I didn't procrastinate for long enough, because David was waiting for me at my locker.

As soon as I saw him, I froze. He leaned against the lockers, his blue blazer draped over his arm. He didn't see me immediately, and for a second, I thought about turning around and running off in the opposite direction.

But then he noticed me, and a bright, large smile came to his face. I felt myself smiling and forced myself to stop. I took a deep breath and marched to my locker.

"Hey," David said as he stood upright and straightened his tie. He looked down at me, but I refused to meet his gaze.

"Hello," I replied as coolly as I could. I opened my locker and began shoving textbooks into my bookbag.

"I tried to call you yesterday."

"I was busy." I peeked at David out of the corner of my eye. A frown had crept upon his face.

I grabbed my last book and slammed my locker shut. "I'd better get out of here. I've got to get to the community center."

"That's it?" David asked. "Is that all you have to say to me?"

"We'll talk more tonight."

I walked off, hoping he wouldn't follow, but of course, he ran up beside me. "Rhonda, what's wrong?"

"Nothing. Like I said before, I've been busy."

David jumped in front of me and forced me to stop. "But we haven't talked all day." He leaned close to me and tried to kiss my cheek, but I sidestepped him.

David sighed. "Is this about Saturday night?"

"Of course not."

"Because if it is, I'm sorry about—"

"I'm going to be late," I said. "I have to go."

I started to back away, but after a couple of steps, David grabbed my hand and pulled me to him. He drew me into his arms, and I momentarily fell in love with him all over again.

"Please tell me what's going on," he whispered.

I choked on my own hesitancy. How could I explain what I was feeling? David was great—almost *too* great. I liked him so much, it was like I had no willpower when I was around him. It was just like when I was with Christopher. And no matter how I felt about David, I couldn't put myself in that situation again.

I pulled myself out of David's arms. "I can't do this."

"What are you talking about?"

I crossed my arms and pretended to be strong. "I don't think you and I are going to work out."

David was quiet for a few seconds. The wrinkles around his eyes exposed his confusion over everything. One minute, we were the perfect couple—the next minute, we were breaking up.

"Rhonda, I'm sorry."

"Stop saying that! It's not your fault!"

"Rhonda—"

"David, please. It was nice while it lasted, but we both knew this relationship wasn't going anywhere. We'll be graduating in six weeks, and three months after that, we'll both be in college."

David's head dropped. He exhaled, and slowly nodded. And just like that, it was done. We were officially over.

"I guess it wasn't meant to be," he said.

I fought back the tears that were trying to escape from behind my eyes. "I guess so."

"But we'll still be friends, right?"

"Of course," I said as my voice began to crack. With every passing second, it was getting harder for me to hold back the tears. As soon as I felt my lips trembling, I knew I had to get out of there.

David must have sensed my fragile state, because he

immediately stepped closer to me. "Maybe if we just talk things over…?"

"Talking won't do any good." I stared at my feet, because I knew I would take back every word I said if I looked at him. "I've made up my mind."

After an eternity of silence, David finally stepped away from me. "Then I'll see you around."

I nodded. "See you around."

I turned and left David standing alone in the hallway. And I was just lucky enough to make it to my car before the floodgates opened and I burst into tears. I thought I would never cry as much as I did when Christopher broke up with me.

I was wrong.

chapter²²
degrees of(freedom)

Although I tried my best to ignore it, I could feel Helen's gaze fixated on me as I flipped through old magazines at her kitchen table. I had come over to her house every other night for the past two weeks—ever since my break-up with David. I had been working on my artwork so much, I was afraid my fingertips would be permanently covered in glue.

"Why are you staring at me?" I finally asked, as I closed a magazine and picked up a catalog.

"You shouldn't be here," Helen said. "It's your prom night."

"I never found a dress."

"Of course you didn't. You stopped looking."

"I didn't have a reason to keep looking, remember."

Helen went back to reading her book. But she couldn't have read more than two words before she slammed the book shut and dropped it on the table.

I sighed. "I guess you want to talk."

Helen's face was almost as red as her hair. "You need to talk to someone. You haven't had a real conversation with your father in over a month. And I bet you haven't said five words to David since y'all broke up."

I frowned. "You should be happy. Things are finally back to normal."

"Things haven't been normal for a long time."

"You know what I mean." I pushed the catalog away from me. "Like I said before I even started dating David, I don't have time for a boyfriend. I have to focus on my grades."

"Rhonda, you made all As last semester."

"I can always do better."

Helen rose from her seat. "And what about your father? He's really trying to reach out to you. But if you don't forgive him, and soon, you're going to lose him."

I rolled my eyes. "I lost my father years ago. Ever since he made me get that abortion—"

Helen slammed her fist on the counter. "Stop using that as an excuse!"

I almost fell out of my seat. "What?"

"It was three years ago. You can't keep using that excuse to push people away." Helen shook her head and muttered to herself as she began pulling pots and pans out of the cabinets.

I walked over to Helen and planted myself behind her. "And why not?"

She slowly turned around, and a crooked, melancholy smile came to her face. "If you keep it up, you'll always be alone."

I dropped my gaze to the floor. "I like being alone."

Helen turned to the stove. "Maybe I should keep my mouth shut. You want to be an adult? You want to make your own decisions? Then go ahead and keep doing what you're doing." She yanked open a drawer and pulled out a fistful of silverware.

"Listen, Helen—"

Before I could continue, the phone rang. Helen slipped past me and picked up the phone. A frown came to her face. "Hey, Gail," she said into the phone. "Do you want to talk to Rhonda?"

After a long pause, Helen's frown deepened. "I see," she said. "Okay, I'll tell her."

By now, I was at Helen's side. But instead of handing me the phone, she hung it up, with a dumbfounded look on her face.

"What's wrong?"

Helen blinked as if she was coming out of a trance. "Grab your keys," she said. "Sarah just went into labor."

∴

I rushed out of the elevator and headed down the white, medicine-filled hallway. My stomach was twisted into a pretzel and my mouth tasted like chalk. Did Sarah really go into labor? Was the baby alright?

I marched toward the nurse's station, but froze once I saw David standing at the counter. I was pretty far away from him, but I could hear his voice booming throughout the hallway. A nurse was standing in front of him, doing her best to calm him down. He just shook his head and slapped his hand against the counter.

I quickened my pace. If David didn't quiet down, he was going to get himself thrown out of the hospital.

"Why can't you tell me anything?" he demanded of the nurse. "They told me she was transferred to a room up here."

The nurse glanced down at a clipboard. She looked like *she* needed to be admitted to a hospital, the way her cheeks hung on her face. She reminded me of a human bulldog.

"Like I said before, I don't have any information at this time." The nurse pointed to a room in the corner. "Why don't you have a seat? I'll let the doctor know you're here."

"But can't I see her now? I'm her brother."

The nurse glared at David. "Listen here—"

"We'll wait for the doctor," I said, raising my voice and stepping beside David. "We're just anxious."

David stared at me for a few seconds, not saying anything. Then he sighed and turned back to the nurse. "We'll wait for the doctor."

The nurse rolled her eyes and left the counter. David looked back at me and smiled nervously.

"Hey," he said, his voice now quiet. He drummed his fingers on the countertop. "You got the message?"

I nodded. "Gail called me a few minutes ago." I looked at his lanky fingers as they tapped against the counter. I almost reached out and grabbed his hand. *Almost.*

"Sorry, I didn't mean to startle you," I continued. "But you were yelling, and—"

"And I needed to calm down," he said. "Thanks."

"That's what friends are for, right?"

We continued to stare at each other. A nuclear explosion could have gone off and we wouldn't have noticed.

"I was playing basketball when I got a message from Sarah," he said. "I got here as soon as I could."

"Playing basketball? You weren't getting ready for the prom?"

He shook his head and smirked. "My date backed out on me."

It took a second, but I finally realized he was talking about me. I frowned and focused my attention on the white, tiled floor.

"I was trying to be funny," he mumbled. "You know, to break the tension."

"Sorry. I didn't get the joke."

This was our first attempt at having a real conversation since the break-up, and we were failing miserably at it. It used to be we could talk about anything. Now, I could have had a more engaging conversation with a pet rock.

"There you guys are."

I turned once I heard Gail's voice. She looked like a throwback to the movie stars of the sixties in her cream and gold, off-the-shoulder prom dress. Xavier looked like…Xavier, only with a better haircut. At least he smelled nice.

Gail floated over to me. "Sarah didn't have Helen's phone number so she asked me to get ahold of you." She turned to David. "Is she having the baby?"

"I don't know," David said. "The doctor will talk to us in the waiting room in a few minutes. We were headed over there now."

Xavier nodded. "That's where we just came from. I think your mother is in there."

David rushed toward the waiting room, with the rest of us in tow. We entered to see his mother sitting on a couch, reading a magazine. She looked just as menacing as she did the last time I saw her, in her office.

We waited by the doorway as he ran over to his mother. "Mom, what happened?"

"I'm not sure," she said. "I got home to see a note on the table saying that she was coming to the hospital." Ms. Gamble glanced back at her magazine and flipped the page. "It's probably nothing. You know how your sister likes to overreact to things."

David shook his head and waved his arms around. "You call this overreacting? She's at the hospital."

Ms. Gamble didn't seem swayed by David's theatrics. "It's probably just Braxton Hicks contractions. I had the same thing when I was pregnant with both you and Sarah."

Even from across the room, I could tell David was nearing his breaking point. He began popping his knuckles and pacing in front of his mother.

Ms. Gamble didn't look up from her magazine. "You're not helping matters."

David stopped. "Can you at least *pretend* to be concerned?"

I went to David and softly placed my hand on his arm. "I'm sure the doctor will be here in a few minutes to tell us exactly what's going on." I slipped my fingers around his. "Sarah's alright. She's one tough little chick."

"Hello, Rhonda," Ms. Gamble said, her words sharp and pointed. "Did you get a full scholarship to Georgia Tech?"

"No, only a partial," I mumbled.

"Hmm," she said, a small smirk on her face. "That's too bad."

I gritted my teeth and squeezed David's hand.

David cleared his throat. "Did you call Dad?"

"Of course not," Ms. Gamble said. "Why would I do that?"

"Sarah would want him to know," he said.

Ms. Gamble's gaze darted from David to me, and then

back to her son. "Since when did you start caring about your father?"

David shrugged. "This isn't about me. This is about Sarah."

Ms. Gamble finally closed the magazine. "I don't know why you're getting so worked up over this." She stood up and fished a pack of cigarettes and a lighter out of her purse. "She wouldn't even be in this situation if she hadn't acted like a tramp and slept around."

David's knees buckled. "Mom…"

"I'm just telling the truth." She pointed her finger at David. "I don't know why you keep standing up for her. She slept around and now she's got to pay the price." She shook head. "Look, she's even got me smoking again."

Ms. Gamble was talking loudly enough for everyone in the room to hear her. Gail and Xavier had stuck their faces in a book, but I knew they were listening.

David's hand felt like dead weight around my fingers, but I didn't let go. "Mom, don't say stuff like that."

"Honey, don't waste your sympathy on her," Ms. Gamble said. "Sarah is just like her father—she only thinks of herself. And if it takes having an illegitimate child for her to learn from her mistakes, then so be it."

Luckily, before Ms. Gamble could say anything else, a doctor entered the room and walked up to David. "I'm Dr. Williams. Are you part of the Gamble family?"

David nodded, and everyone (well, everyone except Ms. Gamble) crowded around the doctor.

"Sarah went into what we call preterm labor," he said. "But we were able to stop the contractions."

"Is she okay?" David asked.

Dr. Williams nodded. "She'll be fine. What we plan to do is put her on limited bed rest and give her medicine to help stave off labor. We'd like her to carry the baby full term, and we think she can do it."

Gail poked Dr. Williams on the arm. "Can we see her?"

"Are you a family member?" he responded.

Gail meekly shook her head.

"I'm sorry, but I can't allow it. Only family is allowed to see patients at this hour."

Ms. Gamble rose from her seat. "When will my daughter be able to go home?"

"Monday morning," he said. "Would you like me to show you to her room?"

She shook her head. "I need to take a smoke break first. Why don't you show David to the room? I'll be there momentarily." Ms. Gamble gave me one final hard glare, and then left the room.

"I guess I'd better go see Sarah," David said. "I wish y'all could come with me."

"It's okay," I said. "Just tell her that we said hello and we'll see her tomorrow." I finally let go of David's hand, and he trudged out of the room behind the doctor.

Gail sighed. "I would have felt better if I could have seen her, but at least she's okay." She glanced at a wall clock. "Maybe we can still make it to the prom."

"How can you think about prom at a time like this?" Xavier asked.

She shrugged. "Do you know how much this dress cost?"

Gail and Xavier continued their banter, but I tuned them out. David and Dr. Williams had only traveled a few feet before David stopped walking. David leaned close to the doctor and whispered something. The doctor stepped back, glanced at his watch, and quickly nodded. David smiled and ran back to the room.

"Come on," he said, grabbing my hand. "I can get you in to see Sarah, but only for a few minutes."

"But how—"

"I informed him that my father's company donated almost a quarter of a million dollars to research hospitals," he said, yanking me behind him. "Now come on. Mom will be back up here pretty soon."

"I'll be back in a second," I yelled to Gail and Xavier as David pulled me down the hallway to where Dr. Williams was standing.

"She can only visit for a few minutes," Dr. Williams said. "Now as I was saying before, I think your father would be most interested in hearing about some equipment we need—"

"I'll talk to him about it," David said, waving off the doctor. "Who do I talk to about picking up Sarah's car?"

Dr. Williams frowned. "Her car? To my knowledge, your sister didn't drive herself to the hospital."

"Of course she did," David said. "I didn't drive her and neither did my mother. Did she call an ambulance or something?"

"No, I think her boyfriend brought her in."

Both David and I froze. "Her boyfriend?" we asked in unison.

"At least I thought it was her boyfriend," Dr. Williams said. "He was carrying on as if he was the father of the child. I only assumed—"

"What room?" David asked, through clenched teeth.

"Room 612, at the end of the hall."

David stormed down the hallway. Unfortunately, his hand was still attached to mine, so I was dragged off behind him. I could almost see the steam rising from David's head. I was glad we were at a hospital, because I was afraid whoever was in that room with Sarah would need serious medical attention after David got to him.

David flung open the door and barged into Sarah's room. "Where the fuck is he?!"

I peeked around David so I could get a better look at Sarah. Her bangs were plastered to her forehead and an IV was hooked into her arm, but otherwise she looked okay. Thankfully, she was the only person in the room.

"I sent him home," she said. "I didn't want you to meet him like this."

I circled David and went to Sarah's bed. "You okay?"

She nodded. "It's nothing a little nap can't fix."

David stormed toward us. "Sarah, are you going to tell me who he is or not?"

I stepped in front of him. "David, calm down. Your sister is in the hospital, for goodness sake."

A flicker of his usual kind self shone through the anger seething from his eyes. "But—"

"Your sister needs you," I whispered.

David shook his head. "But he…he—"

"David, please," I said.

He sighed. "I'm sorry." He took Sarah's hand. "How do you feel? Do you need anything?"

Sarah smiled, and for a brief moment, everything was good in the universe. "I'm okay."

There was a slight rap on the door. I looked up to see Dr. Williams. "Time's up," he said.

I leaned over and smoothened her hair. "Gail and Xavier said to hurry up and get well. We'll come by and see you tomorrow."

Just as I was heading out the door, David grabbed my hand. He looked at me with those powerful hazel eyes of his, and I felt myself turning into putty.

"Can you stick around for a few minutes?"

I frowned and looked at my watch. "It's getting late."

"Please."

I reluctantly nodded. "I'll be in the waiting room."

David released my hand, and I left the room. I made my way back to the waiting room, where Gail and Xavier were still arguing. However, they stopped once they saw me enter the room.

"How is she?" Gail asked.

"She's going to be okay," I said. "She's a little tired, but that's about it."

Xavier pushed Gail out of the way. "How does she look?"

I rolled my eyes. "Still beautiful."

Xavier gave off a sigh of relief and turned to Gail. "*Now* we can go to the prom."

Gail nodded. "Go get the car. I'll meet you out front in a few minutes."

As soon as Xavier left, Gail turned to me and planted her hands on her hips. "What the hell is wrong with you?"

"What?"

"Why did you break up with David? Any idiot can see you still care for him."

"You were the one that said I shouldn't see him in the first place."

"I was wrong," Gail said. "Get your boyfriend back, before it's too late."

I watched Gail saunter out of the room. She didn't realize it, but it was already too late. Some things just weren't meant to be—no matter how much you wanted them.

chapter[23]
if/then(statements)

A few minutes after Gail left, David entered the waiting room. "I'm glad you stuck around," he said. "You want to get a cup of coffee or something?"

I frowned and stuck out my tongue. "How about hot chocolate?"

David nodded, and we headed toward the cafeteria. David ordered coffee, without cream or sugar, and I ordered hot chocolate. He began to pay for both of our drinks, but I stopped him. "I can pay for mine."

David ignored me and handed the cashier a twenty-dollar bill. "I don't mind." He flashed me a smile. "It's not like I'm buying you a diamond ring. It's just a cup of hot chocolate."

We took our drinks and walked to a table in the far corner of the room. Instead of looking at David, I focused on the miniature marshmallows bobbing up and down in my cup.

"Why did you want me to stay?" I finally asked.

"Back in the waiting room, when Mom and I were arguing, you held my hand." David took a sip of his coffee, and sat it back down on the table. "It felt nice."

I disregarded the steam rising from my hot chocolate and poured some into my mouth. It burned my tongue, but I forced it down anyway.

"I like you a lot, Rhonda." He reached across the table and took my hand. "To be honest, I think I—"

"Don't say it," I warned him, my voice unsteady. "You don't even know me."

"But it's true." David intertwined his fingers with mine. "Are you going to sit here and tell me you don't feel the same way?"

I wanted to move my hand from under his, but my arm wouldn't cooperate.

"Why did you break up with me?" he continued. "What did I do that was so wrong?"

"You didn't do anything."

"I had to have done something. Everything was going great, and then all of a sudden, things got weird." He paused to take another drink of coffee. "Just tell me the truth. On that night at my house, I went too far, didn't I?"

I pulled my hand from his. "Will you stop saying that? How many times do I have to tell you, it wasn't because of that."

"Then tell me why. What the hell could I have done to make you break up with me? I thought things were going well. I thought you liked me. I thought—"

"I had an abortion."

David froze, his eyes glazed over, his mouth hanging open.

"It happened a long time ago." My voice was a lot calmer than I expected it to be.

David's eyes were wide and full of remorse. "I'm sorry."

"It wasn't your fault."

"I know it wasn't. I meant…what I was trying to say—"

"You don't have to apologize for something you didn't do."

David busied himself by drinking the rest of his coffee. He was doing his best to look cool and composed, but his trembling hands gave him away.

"It was Christopher's, wasn't it?"

I nodded, and David began to grind his teeth together.

"It happened three years ago. Christopher wasn't mature enough to deal with the situation."

"So he didn't go to the clinic with you?"

"No, Dad did."

David frowned. "Why didn't you make Christopher

own up to his actions? Didn't you tell his parents about the pregnancy?"

I hesitated for a second, before shaking my head. "I promised Christopher I wouldn't," I said. "His father isn't very nice."

David chewed on his lip for a few moments. "I've heard stories about his father before, but I didn't believe them."

"Trust me, everything you've heard is true. I've seen the bruises."

David closed his eyes and tilted his head back. For a few seconds, it seemed like the entire cafeteria was quiet. "Now everything is starting to make sense," he said, looking back at me. "That night, at my house, when things started to heat up…"

"I can't go through that again, David. I *won't* go through that again."

"But I'd never do that to you. I'm not Christopher."

I sighed. "But I'm still Rhonda. And it's not you that I'm worried about. It's me."

David reached for my hand again, but this time I pulled away before he could grab it. "You know, we don't have to have sex."

For the first time that night, I laughed. "I wish I could believe you, but to be honest, I don't trust either of us. Put us in the right situation and I know we'll sleep together." I wearily smiled at him. "We're teenagers. That's what teenagers do."

"But what about condoms?"

"Mistakes can still happen with condoms," I said. "I just can't take that risk."

He shook his head. "Can't we at least try to make this work? I promise, I won't pressure you into having sex."

I crossed my arms. "How many girlfriends have you had since ninth grade?"

David shrugged. "I don't know. Four. Maybe five."

"And how many have you slept with?"

He looked away from me.

"How many?" I demanded. "One? Two?"

David continued to stare at the tabletop.

I sunk a little lower in my seat as the sad truth came to me. "You slept with all of them, didn't you?"

"All of them, except for you."

I didn't know whether to feel vindicated or disappointed. I finished the rest of my hot chocolate and rose from the table. "What would you do if I got pregnant?"

David's eyes widened. "I don't know. I'd marry you, I guess."

"What if I don't want to get married?" I placed my hands on my hips. "What if I don't want to have the baby at all?"

David stood up. "You'd get another abortion?"

I looked at David's sweet, caring face. "I don't know what I'd do," I said. "But I do know that if I'm not in a relationship, I don't have to worry about it."

David slowly nodded. "So it really wasn't my fault that we broke up?"

"Of course it wasn't your fault." I stood on my toes and softly kissed his cheek. "We were over before we even began."

∴

Sarah was in much better condition when Gail, Xavier, and I visited her on Sunday. She was doing so well, the doctor discharged her a day early, on the strict orders that she start bed rest immediately. However, she must have been too drugged up to hear his instructions, because she showed up at school on Monday. I finally caught up with her right before lunch, and was relieved to see she was doing okay.

"How do you feel?" I asked Sarah on our way to the cafeteria. "Do you want me to take you home?"

Sarah rolled her eyes. "Since when did you become my chauffeur?"

"You know you're supposed to be on bed rest." I checked her forehead to see if she was hot. "I can't believe your brother let you come to school."

"My bed rest doesn't start until tomorrow." She smiled. "At least, that's what I told David."

"Sarah…"

"It's just one day," she said. "What's the worst that could happen?"

I started to argue more with her, but before I could, someone pushed past me, spinning me around and almost knocking me over. I turned back toward Sarah to see Johnnie Chang glaring at her, a scowl etched into his face.

"What the hell are you doing here?" he demanded. His voice was low, but forceful.

"Johnnie, calm down." Sarah looked around quickly before stepping closer to him. "This is not a conversation we should be having at school."

"I'll leave you alone, once you explain why you're not at home," he said. "You're not only endangering yourself, but you could be harming our child as well."

My mouth dropped open. *Our child?*

Sarah's hand dropped to her stomach. "Johnnie, stop overreacting."

"I'm the one that took you to the hospital this weekend, remember? If anything happens to you…"

It seemed like my mind was working in slow motion. I knew what I was seeing, but my brain was having a hard time processing the information. It was like I didn't want to believe what was in front of me.

Sarah started to speak, but Johnnie placed his pale fingers on her red lips. "I'm not going to argue about this. You know I'm right."

Sarah stared at him for a few seconds, and slowly nodded. "I promise, this is the last day. I'll go on bed rest tomorrow."

Johnnie sighed, and the wrinkles relaxed around his eyes. "I just don't want you to get hurt."

"I won't hurt myself," she said as she stared deep into

Johnnie's eyes. She almost looked like she was going to fall into him.

I cleared my throat, and they broke their gaze and looked at me. "*He's* the father?"

Sarah winked. "Not who you were expecting, was it?"

Johnnie wrapped his arm around his girlfriend. "It was Sarah's idea to keep it quiet."

"Just for a few more weeks," she said as she pulled away from him. She looked around again. "You know you're not supposed to be talking to me like this here."

He took her hand. "You know I can't help it."

Sarah looked hypnotized as she grinned back at him.

I shook my head and tried not to gawk at Sarah and Johnnie. The way they stared at each other, it seemed like they would spontaneously combust at any second.

"Hey, guys."

All three of us jumped. Johnnie immediately yanked his hand away from Sarah. I clutched my chest and spun around.

David smirked. "Sorry, didn't mean to startle y'all." He walked over and playfully slapped Johnnie on the back. "What are you doing here? You don't have lunch until next period."

His gaze dropped to the floor. "I just felt like skipping class."

David frowned. "Since when do you skip class?" He looked at Sarah, and his grimace deepened. Like Johnnie, she was staring at the floor. Both of their faces were beginning to redden.

David turned to me and crossed his arms. "What happened? Did I interrupt something?"

I shrugged. What else was I supposed do?

Johnnie finally looked up. "David, there's something you should know about Sarah and—"

"Johnnie, don't," Sarah said.

He shook his head. "It's time he found out."

David glared at them, and the frown on his face turned permanent. He took a step closer to Johnnie. "It was you, wasn't it?"

Johnnie didn't back down. "I wanted to tell you earlier, but—"

"I figured it was best that we wait," Sarah interjected. "Johnnie wanted to tell you, but I thought it would be better to break the news to you after the baby was born."

"After the baby was born!" David yelled. A few students turned and looked our way.

My heart began to thunder in my chest. "David, calm down," I said. "You're upset."

"Damn right I'm upset!" By now, a small group was forming around us. Before I knew it, David had dropped his books, grabbed Johnnie by the shoulders, and flung him against the wall.

"You got my sister pregnant, and you didn't even have the fucking guts to tell me?"

"I was going to—"

Before Johnnie could finish his statement, David punched him in the stomach. Johnnie grunted and lurched forward, and David punched him again.

I brought my hand to my mouth and watched as Johnnie slid to the ground.

David towered over Johnnie as the entire cafeteria sat in stunned silence. Then, just as quickly, the room erupted into screams. A group of football players rushed over to us and pinned David's hands behind his back.

"Let me go," he shouted. His voice sounded like it could rip through metal.

I dropped my books and tried to push through the crowd forming around David and Johnnie. As David struggled to break away from the mob of students holding him, Johnnie rolled around on the floor, wheezing for air.

I glanced at Sarah. Her eyes seemed like they were going to pop from their sockets. She looked like she wanted to scream, but no words were coming from her mouth.

The jocks continued to hold David back, no matter how much he struggled. They dragged him away from Johnnie and shoved him against a brick wall. As David's backside hit the wall, it looked like all the air got knocked from his body. I cringed and accidentally bit my tongue.

I nudged Sarah. "Go check on Johnnie," I said. "I'll talk to David."

Still silent, Sarah nodded and inched toward Johnnie. Likewise, I began to force my way through the crowd to get to David.

"Get the principal," someone yelled. "We can't hold him forever."

"I said to let me go," David yelled again as he tried to yank his arms free. "I won't hit him anymore."

I finally elbowed my way to David's side. "Let him go," I commanded to the guys pinning him against the wall. To my surprise, they released him, and he immediately began to fall.

I grabbed his arm and tried to steady him while he got his legs under him. "Are you okay?"

"Of course he's alright. He's not the one who got sucker-punched."

I knew that voice anywhere. I turned around to see Christopher McCullough standing behind me.

Christopher pushed me out of the way and got in David's face. "Man, what the fuck are you thinking?" he asked, poking him in the chest. "What made you hit Johnnie like that?"

David glared at Christopher for a few seconds. Then David slowly turned to me. He locked his eyes with mine, and I knew he wasn't thinking about his sister anymore. David turned his gaze back on Christopher.

And then David hit him.

chapter[24]
rise over(run)

David and I sat in his living room. He was on one side of the room, I was on the other. As far as I was concerned, the more space between us, the better.

"Rhonda, don't you have anything to say?"

"No."

"I guess I really messed up this time, didn't I?"

"Yes, you did."

He sighed. "Thanks for bringing Sarah home."

"Who else was going to? You got suspended, remember."

David began picking at his fingernails. He was probably scraping dried blood from around his cuticles.

The phone rang. "That's probably my father," he said, rising from his seat. "He's going to want to ring my neck."

"Good. You deserve it."

David answered the phone, and immediately I could hear yelling from the other end of the line.

I stood from my seat. "I'm going to check on Sarah."

"Dad, will you calm down for a second?" David yelled into the receiver, before turning toward me. "You can stay," he said, his voice quieter. "I won't be on the phone for very long."

I cut my eyes at him. "I don't want to stay."

Before he could say anything else, I slipped out of the room. As I headed down the hallway, David and his father resumed their shouting match.

"Come in," Sarah said, after I knocked on her door.

I opened the door and slid in. Sarah was in bed with a half-empty glass of orange juice on her nightstand and countless blankets at her feet.

I sat on the bed. "How do you feel?"

"Bored."

Sarah's stomach formed a small mountain underneath her blanket. I resisted the urge to rub on her belly. I had heard pregnant women hated that.

I traced my fingers around one of the squares in Sarah's blanket. "So…"

Sarah blushed. "I guess you want to know how Johnnie and I ended up together."

"I have to admit, out of all the guys I was picturing, his face wasn't the first to come to mind."

Sarah sat up in bed and flung her blanket off her. Her stomach looked even bigger without the covering. "I really didn't get to know Johnnie until this year—we were in trig together." She paused to take a sip of her orange juice. "To be honest, I didn't think he was my type. I like guys with money. I want to be spoiled."

"So what happened to make you change your mind?"

"We started studying together. Every Wednesday, we would meet in a back room at the public library and do our homework. And things stayed like that for a few weeks. Then we went from meeting once a week to three times a week. And then we started meeting every day. And then…well, you can gather the rest."

I laughed. "At least now I understand why your grades were dropping."

Sarah reached out and clutched my hand. "It got to the point that I couldn't stop thinking about him. We would try to study, but we would end up talking about everything *but* math. He made me laugh. He made me think." Sarah's voice was growing animated. She held my hand so tightly, it felt like she was going to squeeze the blood out of my fingers. "I still remember the first time we kissed. We had been slaving away for twenty minutes on a homework problem. When we finally got the answer,

I was so happy, I kissed him. Before I could apologize, he was kissing me back."

I shook my head. "If you liked him so much, why did you keep your relationship a secret?"

"Have you met my mother?" She laughed. "Seriously, I just couldn't deal with Mom and David turning their nose up at Johnnie, like I knew they would."

"But David wouldn't have minded that you were dating him."

Sarah snorted. "David means well, but sometimes he acts less like a brother and more like a parole officer. And as much as he likes Johnnie, David wouldn't have been happy about me hooking up with him." She leaned back. "Now that I think about it, David's the reason why my last two boyfriends broke up with me."

"He can't help it. It's in his nature to take care of you."

"It's in his nature to take care of you as well." Sarah paused for a second. "He really loves you."

"He has a funny way of showing it. Anyway, I don't want to talk about it anymore."

"But—"

Sarah was interrupted by two short raps on her door.

"I know it's you, David," Sarah said. "You can come in."

The door creaked open and David poked his head into the room. "I just got off the phone with Dad," he said. "He's on his way here from Charleston, just to chew me out some more. Maybe I should have waited until the middle of the night to hit Johnnie and Christopher."

David smiled, but neither Sarah nor I smiled back.

"Stop being a jackass," Sarah said. "You had no right to hit Johnnie."

"But he—"

"It was as much my fault as it was his," she said. "Are you gonna hit me, too?"

David's gaze fell to the floor. "But he got you pregnant."

"He's my boyfriend," Sarah said. "No, better yet, he's the father of my child. The father of your niece or nephew. Whether you want to admit it or not, Johnnie is going to have a permanent place in my life, in one way or another."

David walked over to Sarah, leaned over, and kissed her cheek. "I'm sorry."

"You're apologizing to the wrong person," Sarah said, her voice cold.

"You're right, I shouldn't have hit Johnnie." David planted his hand on the bed, inches away from my thigh. "I'll go over to his place tonight and apologize."

Sarah snorted. "That's the least you could do."

I looked at my watch and faked a yawn. "I'd better get out of here."

David turned to me. "You want me to walk you out?"

"No, it's okay," I said, already heading toward the door. "See you tomorrow, Sarah."

Sarah waved goodbye, and I left her room. But I hadn't made it halfway down the hall before I heard a set of footsteps echoing behind me.

"Wait up," David said. "I'll walk you to your car."

I quickened my pace. "Like I said before, I can let myself out."

I plowed through the kitchen and slipped out the back door. The scent of an impending downpour was in the air—large, billowing clouds blocked the stars and the moon. I kept my head down and focused on the path before me, and marched toward my car.

As I threw my books into the trunk, David strode toward me. He positioned himself in front of the driver's side door, making it impossible for me to escape without confronting him.

I shut the trunk and walked to him. "What do you want, David?"

"Don't tell me you're mad at me, too."

"Of course I'm mad at you. You looked like you wanted to kill Johnnie."

"I was upset."

"Upset?" I rolled my eyes and leaned against the car. "More like you were possessed."

"I know. That's why I'm going to see Johnnie—"

"Not just Johnnie," I said. "You need to apologize to Christopher as well."

"You've got to be kidding." He finally moved away from the car door. "I can understand if you're mad about me hitting Johnnie, but Christopher had it coming."

"Why? What did he do to you?"

David fidgeted with the cuff of his shirt. "Christopher is the worst kind of guy."

I folded my arms across my chest. "Don't tell me you're jealous."

"You know I'm not the jealous type." David looked at me like he was searching my eyes for some dark, hidden secret. "Doesn't it make you feel good knowing that I knocked the shit out of Christopher?"

"The last thing I need is another person trying to fight my battles," I said. "I'm past trying to punish Christopher for what he did."

"Yeah, you're punishing me instead."

I narrowed my eyes. "And just what is that supposed to mean?"

"You're not over the abortion," he said. "If you were, we'd still be together."

I shook my head. "That's exactly why I broke up with you. You've only known about my past for three days and you're already throwing it back in my face." I opened my car door. "You're just like Christopher."

"Don't you dare compare me to Christopher."

"Why not?" I began counting off on my fingers. "You play basketball. You sleep around, or did you forget about all of the girls you've had sex with over the last few years."

"I was dating them."

"That doesn't change the fact that you slept with them." I blew a renegade strand of hair out of my face. "You come from a rich and powerful family, just like him. You don't get along with your father, just like him." I glared at David. "You tried to sleep with me, just like him."

David grimaced. "You're forgetting one big difference," he said. "I don't get my girlfriends pregnant and make them get abortions."

My mouth dropped open. His words rang in my ears like church bells. I stepped back for a moment and tried to digest what he had just said.

Then I slapped him.

"Fuck you, David Gamble!" I shoved him in the chest, hard. David stumbled backwards, tripped over his feet, and fell into a bed of roses.

I jumped into my car and slammed the door shut. My hands were trembling so much, I could hardly get my keys out of my pocket. I paused to wipe the tears from my eyes with the back of my hand, and finally jammed the key into the ignition. But before I could start the engine, David opened the passenger side door and slipped into the car.

"Get out!" I yelled, loud enough for the entire neighborhood to hear.

"No."

"David, I'm warning you—"

"You know what, I'm sick of this bullshit. You break up with me because I like you, and *I'm* the bad guy?"

I shook my head. "I don't want to have this conversation."

"Of course you don't. You don't *ever* want to talk."

I started the engine. "Get out of my goddamn car."

"Why won't you talk to me? Why are you pushing me away?"

I didn't bother to wipe the tears away at this point. "Just get out," I moaned. "Please?"

David didn't move, and neither did I. There was a trashy love song on the radio I tried to ignore. The engine hummed, but it wasn't quite loud enough to drown out all of the thoughts bouncing around my head.

Finally, David opened the door and stepped out of the car. But instead of closing the door, he leaned down and peered at me.

"Just so you know, it was you—not me—that ended this," David said. "You're the one that pushed me away."

David closed the door and stepped away from the car. As he stood at the edge of his driveway with his hands stuffed into his pockets, he gave me a cold, haunting look. His eyes stayed on me the entire time as I slowly backed out of his driveway. Even after I pulled onto the street and headed home, I couldn't forget the look on his face. It wasn't a look of sadness, disappointment, or even anger.

It was a look of pity.

chapter[25]
dummy(variables)

On Friday after school, as I had done for the entire week, I headed over to Sarah's house. While she was on bed rest, and while David served his five-day suspension, I was responsible for gathering her homework. Grudgingly, I got David's assignments as well.

After I rang the doorbell for the third time, I glanced at my watch. The television was blaring from inside the house, so I knew someone was home. Plus, when I called earlier to let Sarah know I was dropping by, she said David would be home to let me in.

I was about to pound on the door when it swung

open. Sarah stood at the doorway, wearing a pair of plaid pajamas, her hair stuffed into a red bandana.

"What are you doing out of bed?" I asked as I entered the house. "Where's David?"

"He left as soon as he heard you were coming over."

"Good," I said. "I'm in no mood to see him."

"Rhonda, you guys have been avoiding each other all week. Don't you think—"

"Drop it," I warned her as I followed her into her room.

"But I don't understand. Christopher is an asshole—you'd be the first person to admit that." Sarah crawled into bed. "The only problem with him getting punched was that it should have been your fist instead of David's."

"David trying to *save* me by hitting Christopher is just like Dad forcing me to get an abortion. They both need to realize that I can take care of myself."

"He only did it because he loves you."

"He's not my boyfriend. It's not his place to protect me." I unzipped my bag and pulled out a folder. "What do you want me to do with these assignments?"

"I guess that means you don't want to talk about David anymore." Sarah pointed to her desk. "Stick them over there."

Sarah's desk was littered with a mix of fashion magazines and baby books. I pushed a pile of papers to the side and placed her homework on top of the sandalwood veneer.

There were also a few pictures of Johnnie on her desk.

With her secret out in the open, she was free to show off mementos of their relationship. Maybe Johnnie really did love her. Maybe Sarah loved him back. Maybe things would work out for the best after all.

Sarah noticed me looking at her pictures. "Johnnie was pretty mad at David, but he's already over it...unlike *some* people."

I crossed my arms and frowned as I sat on the corner of her bed.

"I think getting beat up hurt Johnnie's pride more than anything," Sarah continued, as she glanced across the room at one of the pictures on her desk. "Johnnie is too much of a nice guy to stay mad at David forever."

"And what about Christopher?"

Sarah's brow furrowed. "You haven't heard? Christopher is pressing charges."

I felt like I just got hit by a truck. "What? You can't be serious!"

Sarah pulled her bandana from her head and ran her fingers through her hair. "He hired some fancy-ass lawyer. They called yesterday and broke the news."

My pulse quickened. "David could lose his scholarship. Hell, he could go to jail."

"He won't go to jail—our lawyer can assure that much," Sarah said, although I could hear the uncertainty in her voice. "He may lose his scholarship, but with his trust fund, he can afford to go to almost any school."

"But it's too late to get accepted to any decent college,"

I yelled, my voice rushed. "And even if he did get accepted somewhere, he couldn't play basketball."

"Rhonda, you're not telling me anything I don't already know."

"Then why are you acting so damn complacent?" I jumped up and pumped my fists. "You guys can't let Christopher get away with this. David has to do something."

Sarah smirked. "For someone that isn't your boyfriend, you seem pretty protective of him."

I rolled my eyes and sat on my hands to keep them still. "Maybe your mother and Christopher's dad can work something out."

"She already tried," Sarah said. "No deal."

"Maybe Christopher will change his mind."

Sarah snorted. "We both know better than that."

I couldn't believe Christopher was actually going to press charges. People got into fights all the time—only spoiled rich kids like Christopher would actually stoop low enough to pull something like this.

I rose from the bed and grabbed my bag. "I'll call you later. I'm heading to Christopher's house."

"Not without me, you aren't."

Sarah pushed the covers off her swollen feet and kicked her legs over the edge of the bed.

"But your doctor said—"

"Screw the doctor," she said. "I'm going. And we should stop by and pick up Gail. She hates Christopher almost as much as you do."

I watched Sarah slip into her jacket. The truth be told, I could probably use all the support I could get.

"Okay, fine," I said. "Let's go save David."

∴

Sarah, Gail, and I pulled up to Christopher's house. It was a huge five-bedroom structure that made the Gamble residence look like a log cabin. Its size alone was intimidating, without taking into consideration the people who lived inside. To make things worse, the infamous black Saab sat in the front yard, taunting me.

"Um…what's the game plan again?" Gail asked. She had been in the middle of eating dinner when we arrived unannounced at her house. We didn't even give her a chance to put on a real pair of shoes before we whisked her out the door.

Sarah slapped her hands together. "We go in there and kick his ass—that's the game plan."

Gail frowned. "Isn't that what got us in this situation in the first place?"

I was beginning to wonder if this was such a good idea. I had no clue what I was going to say to Christopher. All I knew was that he was hurting David, and I was going to do whatever necessary to save my boyfriend.

I mean, my *ex*-boyfriend.

I parked and turned off the engine. "Just follow my lead, okay?"

I felt myself shaking as I got out of the car. I didn't know why I was so nervous. I had been to Christopher's house hundreds of times. Of course, the last time I was here was under worse circumstances than this.

It was right after we broke up. I was a scared, pregnant, fifteen-year-old girl who was still in love with her ex-boyfriend. I felt pathetic as I begged and pleaded with him to come back home with me so we could break the news to my father. As terrified as I was of being pregnant, I was even more scared of telling Dad by myself.

But telling my father about my pregnancy was not in Christopher's plans. First Christopher suggested I got pregnant on purpose, just to win him back. Then he claimed I was easy, and that it could be anyone's baby. The last thing he did was stuff a wad of bills in my hand before shoving me out of the house and slamming the door in my face.

I strode to the front door and rang the doorbell. A chorus of bells chimed throughout the house.

Sarah popped her knuckles. "Rhonda, you go for his head. I'll go for his stomach."

Gail rolled her eyes. "Please tell me you don't plan on fighting this guy."

Before I could reply, the colossal wooden door opened, bringing me face to face with my nemesis. Christopher didn't look surprised to see me. He stood in the doorway, chewing on a bright green apple. His neck muscles bulged with every bite he took. His sleeveless T-shirt showed off his massive arms.

"I knew you would show up," he said in between bites. "I guess you're here to convince me to let your ex-boyfriend off the hook." He frowned at Sarah and Gail. "And I see you brought back-up."

"Can we come in?" I asked. My voice sounded weaker than I wanted it to be.

Christopher looked over his shoulder before turning back to us. "Make it quick. I'm busy."

Christopher stepped back and let us into the house, and I saw what he had glanced at. Christopher's newest conquest, a cute, tanned blonde, sat on the couch. She didn't go to school at Piedmont—for all I knew, she could have been a college student.

The girl stood and extended her hand. "Hi, I'm Anne—"

"Don't bother introducing yourself," Christopher said. "I just need to talk to these girls for a few minutes, and then you'll never see them again."

The blonde, looking confused, just stared as Christopher led us out of the room and into the kitchen.

Christopher smirked at us. "Anne's a freshman. In college."

I shrugged. "I don't care where you scrounged up Bambi. I just want to talk about David."

He took another bite of his apple. "I'm not going to let David get away with hitting me like that. We're taking him to court." Christopher's lip was still red from where David had punched him.

Sarah started toward him. "You jackass—"

I stepped in front of Sarah. The last thing I needed was a pregnant girl trying to pick a fight.

"But why sue?" I asked. "They offered to settle."

"This isn't about the money," he said. "This is about the *principle* of the matter."

I closed my eyes and took a deep breath. "Christopher, please don't do this. David was just angry. It was a mistake."

Christopher finished the last of the apple and tossed the browning core into the wastebasket. "That's not my problem."

I had heard those words before. I tried to think of something else to say, another way to appeal to what little decency he had, but my mind was coming up blank.

"But Christopher—"

"I'm through talking about it." He crossed his arms, flexing his biceps. "I think it's time for you to leave…unless you can think of another way to convince me to drop the charges."

"God, you make me sick." The way his words slithered out of his mouth made me feel violated. "If you're so adamant on taking David to court, why did you even let us in? You could have told us that at the door."

He sneered. "I just wanted to see you beg."

Both Sarah and I gasped, and Gail headed toward him. "Oh, that's it," Gail said, kicking off her sandals. "Let's all beat his ass."

I gathered my wits quickly enough to cut Gail off from reaching him. "Cool down, both of you," I said. "Let me handle this."

"By the way, when did you start dating again?" Christopher asked. "If you were looking for some action, you should have given me a call."

My fingers balled into fists. "Shut up, Christopher."

"Or what?" He puffed out his chest and advanced toward me. "You gonna hit me?"

I was afraid that was exactly what I was going to do.

"I bet you told David we used to be together. From the way he swung at me, he must really hate me." He winked. "You must have been bragging about me."

My forearm began to tremble. I was losing my battle with self-control.

Christopher was in my face at this point, still trying to egg me on. "You had to know that you and David wouldn't last. He's just like me."

And that's when it hit me. My mouth dropped open, and I stared at Christopher like I was seeing him for the first time. Watching him stand there, gloating like a pompous jackass, made me realize I had been a fool for comparing David to him. David would never try to intentionally hurt me like Christopher was doing. David would never abandon me like Christopher had.

David loved me, even when I was too scared to love him back.

I tossed my head back and laughed sarcastically at

Christopher. "You're pathetic," I said. "You're not going to press any charges."

Christopher looked taken aback by my laughter. "Since when do you have the authority to tell me what to do?"

I wagged a finger at him. "You aren't going to press charges," I said again, as if he didn't hear me the first time. "Not unless you want the world to know you got me pregnant."

Christopher's face dropped. "You can't prove that."

"I don't have to prove it."

"You're bluffing," he stammered. "You'd admit to the entire world you had an abortion?"

"Watch me." I spun around and marched past Sarah and Gail, both of them wearing the same dumbfounded expression. I could hear hurried footsteps behind me as I charged into the living room.

Anne rose from the couch as I strode up to her and planted myself in her face. "Listen, girl," I began, "I hate to tell you this, but I hope you have a lot of money saved up. Christopher is stingy when it comes to paying for abortions."

Christopher burst into the living room, with Sarah and Gail a few steps behind him. "Rhonda, what the hell are you doing?"

Anne looked like her feet were glued in place. She quickly glanced from me to Christopher, and then back to me. "I beg your pardon…"

"You heard me. Christopher made me get an abortion

three years ago, and not only did he refuse to come to the clinic with me, he didn't even give me enough money to pay for it."

"He didn't pay for my abortion, either," Sarah chimed in, rubbing her stomach. "That's why I'm pregnant with little Christopher now."

Anne's eyes widened as she looked at Christopher. "You're having a baby?"

"Of course not," he yelled. "Don't believe a word these crazy bitches are saying."

Gail placed her hands on her hips and started whipping her neck back and forth. "You weren't calling me a crazy bitch last month, when you were up in my bedroom, sweating all over my sheets."

Anne looked at Gail. "Did he get you pregnant as well?"

Gail shook her head. "Worse. This fool gave me syphilis."

Christopher looked like he wanted to cry. He rushed to his girlfriend's side. "Anne, I promise, I am not having a kid." He glared at Gail. "And I've never even slept with her, much less given her any diseases."

Anne pointed to me. "And what about her?"

Christopher's mouth dropped open. "I...I..."

That was all Anne needed to hear. She pushed him away and stormed toward the door. "You fucking pig."

Christopher shuffled behind her. "Okay, I asked her to

get an abortion. But I swear, I gave her enough money for the procedure."

I rolled my eyes. "Yeah, like *that's* going to make her take you back."

Anne already had her purse and was halfway out the door. "Listen, I don't know what the hell is going on here, but it's obvious you've got a lot of skeletons in your closet. Do me a favor and lose my number."

The door slammed shut, and the entire house was quiet for a few seconds.

I snapped my fingers. "Damn, I forgot to tell her about the whole premature ejaculation thing." I sighed. "I guess there's always next time."

Gail, Sarah, and I looked at each other and exploded into laughter.

"You enjoyed that, didn't you?" Christopher yelled as he started toward me. "You're such a bitch."

I did my best to stifle my laughter. "What are you going to do, Christopher? Hit me?"

A moment of clarity crossed his face. "You know what, I didn't like that girl anyway. I'll have another girlfriend by the end of the month." He shrugged. "You can't tell everyone I date about our history."

"I'm not worried about your little girlfriends," I said. "I'll tell your father. I'll tell your church congregation. I'll tell the entire goddamn city if I have to." I stepped toward Christopher. "Think of what your father would do if he found out his perfect, God-fearing son not only got me pregnant, but that he gave me the money to get an abortion."

"That's not fair." For the first time that night, Christopher looked scared. "You know how I feel about my father."

Christopher hadn't changed. He was still afraid of his father, and rightfully so. Unfortunately for Christopher, his home life was no longer my concern.

"Wasn't your father promising to send you to the military if you screwed up again?" My lips curled into a sadistic smirk. "The Marine Corps, right?"

"You bitch—"

"You really need to expand your vocabulary," Gail said. "Haven't you ever heard of a thesaurus?"

Christopher growled, his eyes ablaze with anger. "You goddamn... *bitches.*"

That just made us laugh even more.

I shook my head and tisked. "You should have thought about that before you got me pregnant." I crossed my arms. "You're not going to press charges."

Christopher looked at all of us, his mouth twisted into a snarl. He fixated his gaze on me, doing his best to stare me down.

I stared back, not blinking once.

Christopher finally sighed, and his body relaxed. "Fine, I won't press charges. Now get the fuck out of my house."

I felt like I had won a heavyweight boxing match. I

knew I was leaving on my own terms, with my head held high. My dignity was intact. I was even able to take a chunk of Christopher's self-esteem with me, and that alone was better than any punch I could have thrown. Why hit him with my fists when words stung even more?

Maybe I had learned something important from Christopher after all.

Christopher escorted us outside. I could feel the anger bubbling just under the surface of his skin. I let Sarah and Gail walk ahead of me, slowing enough so Christopher and I could talk privately.

I flashed him a genuine smile. "You know, Christopher, I need to thank you. I had a lot of pent-up anger about our whole situation. Now, I feel like I can finally get some closure."

He grimaced. "I'm glad you took such enjoyment from making my life miserable."

"Making *your* life miserable?" I shook my head. "What I put you through tonight doesn't even compare to what you did to me."

I noticed an array of colorful rocks surrounding a bed of azaleas at my feet. "I heard your mom got a new SUV. She gave you the Saab, right?"

"Um…yeah," Christopher mumbled. "Why do you care?"

"Oh, no reason." I leaned over and picked up a palm-sized rock.

Christopher frowned. "What are you going to do with that?"

I held the rock to my face and bounced it in my hand. *Good size. Good weight.*

"Your father is a mean asshole, and I'm sorry you have to live with him. That's the only reason I've protected you for this long."

"Well, now I guess we're even."

"Humiliating you in front of your girlfriend had nothing to do with us. That was strictly about David." I stole a glance at the Saab out of the corner of my eye. It didn't look so high and mighty anymore.

I turned toward the car and cocked my arm. "This is for me."

I slung my arm forward and threw that rock as hard as I could. Everything moved in slow motion as the rock sailed gracefully from my hand. It arched just right, and came swooping down toward the back window of the car.

Then there was the perfect sound of glass shattering, accompanied by the shriek of the car alarm.

Christopher didn't know whether to rush toward his car or toward me. He narrowed his eyes and glared at me. "You...you..."

I waved him off. "Yeah, yeah, I know. I'm such a bitch. You've only said that twenty times tonight." I lowered my voice and leaned closer to him. "But I promise, if you don't drop the charges, I'll really show you how much of a bitch I can be."

I winked at him and strutted to my car. I could feel his gaze on me the entire time. After opening the door, I turned back to him. "Oh yeah...*now* we're even."

Seconds later I was cruising down the street, a huge smile plastered on my face. And if I listened really hard, I could still hear the car alarm wailing in the background.

chapter²⁶
inflection(points)

Sarah and Gail wanted to go out and celebrate our victory over Christopher, but I had more important plans. I dropped Gail off at her house, took Sarah back home, and parked myself in her living room. I wasn't leaving until I talked to David. I knew he was out playing ball and that he may not be home until late, but I didn't care. I wasn't leaving. I wasn't running away. Not this time.

David was right. I had been pushing—no, more like shoving—him away from me. If he had the guts to love someone as screwed up as me, I should at least be brave enough to try to love him back. That is, *if* he took me back.

As I sat there, surrounded by the calm of the darkness, I thought of all the reasons why I loved David. He was sweet. He made me feel safe. He loved me, even when I hated him.

He tried to save me from myself, even when I didn't know I needed rescuing.

The funny thing was, the longer I sat there, the less I thought about David. Not that I didn't want to make up with him—there was just a greater reconciliation I had been postponing for way too long. Three years, to be exact.

David cared for me, but there was a man that loved me even more. A man brave enough to make the decisions I couldn't bring myself to make, and strong enough to carry the burden of the mistakes I couldn't bear alone.

I thought about calling home, but before I could summon the courage to pick up the phone, I heard David's car pull into the driveway.

My stomach immediately twisted itself into a knot. I would have given anything for a bottle of water at that moment to quench my suddenly dry throat. I was so uptight, I thought I was going to snap in half.

I wiped my glasses on my shirt and stuck them back on my nose as David unlocked the door and slipped into the house. He dropped his basketball by his feet and turned to lock the door.

"Hey," I said.

David spun around. Although it was dark, I could still

make out the perplexed look on his face. "Rhonda, is that you?"

I stood from the couch and held my hands behind my back, so he couldn't see them shaking. I took a hesitant step toward him. "I was waiting on you."

David continued to stand by the door. "Why are you here?" he asked, his words short. "It's late."

I moved to the middle of the room. David remained at the door, which was okay. It was my turn to come to him. "Why did you hit Christopher?"

"Why do you care?"

I could feel the intensity of his gaze on me. I briefly closed my eyes and took a few deep breaths. "At first I thought you were jealous," I said. "But you weren't, were you?"

I was near enough to see David's body tense up. I inched closer to him.

"And you didn't hit Christopher because you were angry at him, did you?"

His jaw stiffened. "I was pretty damn upset."

"But that's not why you hit him."

David pursed his lips together and slowly nodded. "That's not why I hit him."

Two steps later, I was standing right in front of him. He had to be able to hear my heart beating through my chest.

"You did it for me, didn't you?"

David shrugged. "I just thought...it seemed like—"

I placed my fingers on David's lips to stop his rambling.

"Since I couldn't punish Christopher, you tried to do it for me."

David's stance relaxed. He looked at me, and I almost lost myself in his eyes. "It seemed like you needed closure," he whispered.

"I did."

We stayed silent for a few moments, just staring at each other. For as scared and unsure and timid as I felt, I also felt…happy. My heart was aching, but in a good way.

"So now what?" he asked.

I wearily smiled. "Now you let me take you out tomorrow night."

David shook his head. "I don't know…"

No way was David getting away that easy.

I stepped even closer to him, so that his personal space was now my personal space. "You know I like you?"

Finally, a smile crept onto David's face. He nodded.

I took off my glasses. "And I know you like me, right?"

He nodded again, with a grin large enough to brighten the entire room.

I reached up and pulled his face toward mine. "So if you don't mind, I'm going to kiss you now, before I lose my nerve."

So I closed my eyes and kissed him like I was kissing him for the first time. And maybe it *was* the first time, because he had never kissed this Rhonda before. Yeah, maybe I looked the same in his eyes. And yeah, maybe my lips still felt the same against his lips. But there was one thing I could do now that the old Rhonda could have never done.

I could accept true love and return it exponentially.

(remainders)

There have been a plethora of math-related sayings used over the years, ranging from René Descartes' "Perfect numbers like perfect men are very rare," to the oft-used quip, "Life is too short for long division." Given my problems with the verbal portion of the SAT, I was a big fan of a quote by Nathanael West: "Numbers constitute the only universal language."

Wouldn't it be great if every person, every event that had ever taken place, could be simplified into a series of small mathematical formulas? Why spend pages and pages of text describing the details of someone's life, when you-could scribble down a few lines of equations that quantified things just as easily?

For instance, if I had to summarize my life after Piedmont, it would be something like this:

Partial scholarship + Dad footing the rest of the bill
$$= \text{Georgia Tech}$$
Sarah Gamble $\cup$ Johnnie Chang = 8 lb., 3 oz. baby boy
$$\equiv \text{David Lee Chang}$$
(Xavier + perky, seventeen-year-old lifeguard) x 3 dates
$$= 1 \text{ used condom}$$
Christopher $-$ 2 credit hours needed to graduate +
$$1 \text{ underage DUI} = \text{Marine Corps}$$
Justice Gamble + new grandson = Bitch x 50%
Gail + 4.0 GPA = valedictorian
Dad + Jackie = wedding bells
Dad + Rhonda $\approx$ 1 normal family
David + Rhonda $\rightarrow \infty$!
$|\text{Rhonda} + \text{friends} + \text{family}| = \text{Happiness}^2$

Not quite Shakespeare, but it should do just fine.

Q.E.D. (THE END)

© Kenneth Gall

About the Author

Growing up, Varian Johnson couldn't decide whether he wanted to be an engineer or a writer, so he decided to do both. Born and raised in Florence, South Carolina, he now lives in Austin, Texas with his wife and two cocker spaniels. In preparation for this novel, Varian memorized π to the tenth decimal place, relearned how to triple integrate a fifth-order polynomial, and bought his first home pregnancy kit. Check him out at www.varianjohnson.com for more interesting, but totally useless, information.

Q + A
With Varian Johnson

1. *Can you tell us a little bit about where* My Life as a Rhombus *came from? So much happened in Rhonda's life before the book begins, so it seems like the book must have had quite a complicated genesis.*

My Life as a Rhombus was inspired by a friend I met a few years ago. The young woman already had one child (an eight-year-old) and upon discovering that she was pregnant again, she eventually decided to have an abortion.

My friend had a decent job, but she still struggled to make ends meet. More times than not, she had to depend on friends or parents when money got tight. So from her point of view, she had no choice but to terminate her pregnancy. Any other option would have been unfair to the daughter she already had.

What really resonated with me was that when I offered to go to the clinic with her, she declined. She said that it wasn't my place; it wasn't my responsibility. She had gotten herself into this predicament and now it was up to her to get herself out of it.

While Rhonda isn't in the same situation as my friend, I was intrigued with just how much my friend wrestled with her options—and how she repeatedly reminded me that I wasn't there to fix her problem, just to listen.

I wondered what would have happened if she hadn't had the abortion. I wondered what would have happened if she had been forced to make a decision that she wasn't quite comfortable with.

2. *There are fewer men who write for young adults than women, and very few men who write first-person female narrators. Why did you choose to do this? What were some of the challenges?*

I originally considered writing this as an adult novel, from Rhonda's father's point of view. But very quickly, I realized that if anyone was going to tell this story, it would be Rhonda. I also realized that in order for the reader to truly understand what Rhonda had gone through, I had to write the novel in first-person.

Of course, I've never been a teenage girl, much less a

teenage girl who had once been pregnant, so I knew I was up for quite the challenge when I began the novel. I conducted a lot of research on pregnancy and abortion—and not just medical research. It was important for me to dig deep and to research a teenager's emotional response to pregnancy and abortion.

3. *You're also an engineer—the career Rhonda aspires to. Is there a little bit of you in Rhonda? How do engineering and writing books for teens intersect—if they do at all?*

Rhonda's a math geek—of course there's a bit of me in her (although, for better or for worse, I'm probably more like her father). Engineering and writing are both similar, at least in a few ways. Both take a lot of creativity and determination. Both usually take years and years to master. But if I had to pick, I'd say that writing is much more difficult than engineering. The rules of science and math are very exact. The rules of writing, on the other hand, are guidelines at best. What's right for one book can be completely wrong for another.

4. *Was it important to you to write an African-American protagonist who faced challenges aside from race? What about the character of Justice Gamble?*

I do think that it's important to feature African-American characters who are not purely defined by race. We live in a diverse society where decisions are influenced by number of factors: socio-economic status, political affiliation, religious beliefs, educational level, and of course, ethnicity. While I'm proud to be an African-American, my race doesn't dictate every decision I make. Likewise, the same should hold true for Rhonda and her father.

However, I feel that I have an opportunity—or perhaps even a responsibility—to create fiction that positively portrays aspects of the African-American experience. Is it really that unbelievable for Justice Gamble to sit on the South Carolina Supreme Court? I'd bet that the Honorable Ernest A. Finney, Jr. (South Carolina's first African-American Supreme Court Justice) may disagree.

I'm not saying that race isn't important. I'm just saying that it's not important all the time. I promise, when Rhonda was waiting for the results of her pregnancy test, the last thing on her mind was her ethnicity.

5. *In a similar vein, you've written a book where abortion is an important issue, but your book doesn't take an explicit pro- or anti-choice position. It's not a preachy or political novel, but it is very frank about choices and their consequences. Did you set out to write a book "about abortion" or was abortion more of a vehicle to allow you explore a character?*

I never intended to write a novel that either validated or opposed abortion. If anything, the novel is about the power of forgiveness (hokey, but true).

That being said, I knew I was walking into a potential

hotbed when I decided to use abortion as the main plot device. But I think that's what writers are supposed to do. A lot of the time, the issues that a character struggles with are some of the same issues that the author himself has struggled with.

Personally, I've always struggled with the legal and moral aspects of abortion. I hoped that writing this novel would help me sort out my position on the matter. If anything, all I've realized is that it's a hell of a lot easier to be pro-life or pro-choice when you aren't the one who can get pregnant.

6. *Care to talk a little about the challenges and rewards of writing for teens? You're still a young guy. Are you just working out your issues with your own teenage years?*

I love looking at life through a teen's eyes. Teenagers see the world through such a clear lens—before things like work, bills, and family begin to clutter their landscape. Also, teens know crap when they see it, and nowadays, they aren't afraid to tell you so. You've got to get the story— their story—right, and in the process of telling their story, you have to respect them.

As for myself, I don't have any residual issues from my teenage years. I'm nothing like the teenagers I write about. I was a good, obedient, perfect kid. At least, that's what I tell my parents.

7.   Any advice for aspiring writers?

Read as much as you can. Read the classics, but also read contemporary works, because industry standards fluctuate. Read books both within and outside your genre. Read, read, read.

Then, write. Every day. Writing is about putting "butt in chair" and putting "words on paper." The revision can come later; the first draft is all about getting the story on the page.